# MOORE THAN ENOUGH

## All That & Moore Book 7

---

## CELESTE GRANGER

Want to be in the know? Subscribe to my newsletter to be a part of Celeste Granger's Tangled Romance!
https://landing.mailerlite.com/webforms/landing/k2e1j4
Follow me on Facebook @ https://www.facebook.com/TheCelesteGranger/
Want to join my reading group, Reading with Celeste?
Follow the link: https://www.facebook.com/groups/1943300475969127/

## Acknowledgment

I hope you don't get tired of reading it because I will never stop saying it. I am so grateful for each of you. There are so many books you could have read, so many authors you could support, and you choose to support me. That support doesn't go unnoticed. I appreciate every Facebook mention, and I appreciate every like love and share. I appreciate you being there for me. It's not easy being a writer. This industry is challenging, and writing can be isolative at times. But you make every early morning and every late-night worth it. Thank you!

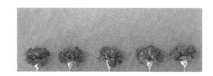

*This book is dedicated to every friend that became a lover and more.*

# Chapter One

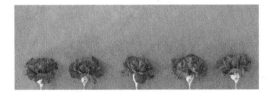

*A*mbient light filled the intimate space. It was just the two of them. The soothing scent of vanilla warmed the room as low candlelight highlighted their silhouettes. She stood in front of him in all her glory, the well of her full breasts pressing against him.

"Uhn," she moaned against his muscular chest. He held her in the strength of his chiseled arms and rocked her as the next contraction crested.

"You are doing so well, beautiful," Bryce hummed against Kennedy's neck as she cradled her head snugly against him.

Bryce could feel the swell of her belly against him as Kennedy moaned again. Knowing that she carried his seed in her precious womb made Bryce proud and scared simultaneously. He hated to see Kennedy in so much pain. She'd been in labor for hours, and the baby seemed no closer to being ready to come. He prayed for her as he rocked her.

Bryce couldn't wait to see the child that was conceived out of love, but he also needed for Kennedy to be okay, too. She was everything to him. Kennedy completed Bryce in ways he could have never imagined, and he didn't want to consider living the rest of his life without her. There were so many women who lost their lives in childbirth. It was tragic and unfortunate for anyone. Bryce didn't want the love of his life to be one of them. As Kennedy's hips swayed back and forth, Bryce did whatever he had to do to support her. When she was thirsty, Bryce made sure Kennedy had water to drink. When her back hurt, he massaged it until she felt better. And when she cried from exhaustion and weariness, Bryce wiped the tears from her eyes. She was in so much pain. Kennedy's pain was Bryce's pain. He felt her body convulse under the strain of the contractions.

"Uhn," Kennedy groaned again.

"I wish I could take the hurt away," Bryce crooned as Kennedy held him tightly, riding the crest of yet another contraction.

A smile eased across Kennedy's lips as she looked up into the face of her handsome husband.

"You can't have it," Kennedy smiled. "This pain makes me a mom," Kennedy sighed as a well of emotion surged inside her soul. "And you a dad. Can you believe it, bae? We're gonna be parents."

Just as Kennedy felt a well of emotion blossoming inside her, Bryce found himself choking back the tears. Even in pain, she touched him. She had the audacity to smile through it all.

"You know I love you," Bryce chortled as he nestled his

lips against the length of Kennedy's neck, kissing her lovingly.

"I know," Kennedy smiled. But the beauty of her smile quickly changed into a grimace as sharp pains shot through her core.

"Oh, my Gawd," Kennedy cried out.

Bryce's eyes widened.

"Sweet! You okay?"

"Uh, uh, uh," Kennedy panted.

Bryce wasn't sure what to do to help her. They'd gone through all the Lamaze classes together. They regularly practiced their breathing exercises and did everything they thought possible to prepare for this very moment. Yet, hearing the hurt and seeing the never-ending discomfort his wife was in, made Bryce feel helpless. All the things they learned went out of the window, and Bryce was nervous. But he had to pull it together. He had to help Kennedy.

"Come on, babe," Bryce encouraged. "Breathe with me."

He had to put his own fears and concerns aside and focus on Kennedy. She groaned again, and Bryce felt her body giving way in his arms. Bryce's heart skipped a beat. He held Kennedy tightly and lifted her slowly, steadying her with his own strength. Once he felt Ken regain her legs, and her breathing began to even out, Bryce captured her eyes with his.

"You ready, sweet," Bryce hummed as they connected. The dark stillness of Bryce's eyes and the strength of the hold he had on her gave Kennedy such a feeling of safety and security. She felt like she could do anything.

"Yeah, babe," Kennedy uttered as the contraction started to wane. "I'm ready."

She gazed into her husband's eyes and found solace there. Together, they breathed in deeply and exhaled slowly. Bryce rubbed Kennedy's hips and lower back as they breathed in together again. The two were in sync; inhaling and exhaling as one. As Bryce looked down into Kennedy's dark irises, he remembered why he fell in love with her in the first place. Ken's eyes were certainly the window to her brilliant soul. She was his comfort and the joy of his life. Just as he was her peace, Kennedy was his peace.

She could start to feel her pelvis relax, and the baby settle down as they inhaled together once again. Kennedy's eyes lit up as she saw a gentle smile move across Bryce's sensual lips. Yes, he was her peace.

"CAN YOU BELIEVE IT? KEN IS HAVING A BABY," IVORY COOED.

"It's surreal," Trinity sighed.

Ivory and Trinity were the youngest two Moore girls. There hadn't been a child born to the family since Trinity's birth more than twenty years ago. Ivory was young at the time so much of it she didn't remember. Now, though, both Ivory and Trinity were grown women, and neither could wait to witness what experiencing a new life in the family would be like.

"Look at mom," Ivory said, directing Trinity's attention to the kitchen.

The entire family was gathered at Bryce and Kennedy's home. Their sister decided to have a home birth with a doula. She wanted the intimacy, and familial setting that only a home birth could provide, and her entire family, as well as Bryce's, was there for it.

Felicia was piddling. She couldn't help it. Although Kennedy and Bryce's kitchen was immaculate, Felicia found ways to keep herself busy by cleaning what was already clean. She couldn't help it. Every time she thought about the miracle transpiring just overhead, her heart swelled, and her eyes teared. The thought of becoming a grandmother was overwhelming. The thought of her daughter laboring to become a mother rendered Felicia speechless. When anyone asked if she was okay, Felicia's eyes brimmed with tears ready to fall to her flushed cheeks. She was just so grateful.

Cecil watched as his wife of more than thirty years wiped counters that were already pristine, rearrange the dishes in the cabinet and sweep the floor that didn't have a speck of dust on it. He didn't say anything. Felicia had her own way of working through things, and Cecil learned during the time they'd been together just to be there if he was needed. Cecil had his own emotions to deal with, too. For the first time in his life, he was going to be a grandfather. A smile brightened his eyes and eased across his lips as he considered what his grandchild might call him. Lifting himself from the stool he'd been sitting on, Cecil padded over to Felicia, who was wiping the stove top for the second or third time. He eased up behind Felicia and wrapped his thickly corded arms around her taut waist. Instantly, Felicia was comforted by his closeness. She exhaled a breath she didn't even realize she'd been holding and settled the back of her head on Cecil's expansive chest.

"What do you think," Cecil's baritone voice drummed. Felicia could feel the reverberation of his deep voice move through her as he spoke. "Papa or Pop?"

Turning on her heels, Felicia spun in his arms to face him. His was a face Felicia loved. Cecil had been not only an incredible husband, but he was also an amazing father to their eight girls. Felicia found herself ever grateful for the man Cecil was to her and their daughters.

"What about Poppy?" Felicia purred with a wink and a smile. Even though she was on the verge of tears, Cecil had a way of keeping her smiling.

"Oh, I don't think so," Cecil gently rebuffed, squeezing Felicia tightly and drawing her closer into him.

"Why not," Felicia teased.

"Because only you can call me that."

There was a knowing glance the two shared, and Felicia's eyelashes fluttered as she blushed. Leaning down, Cecil kissed Felicia on the forehead, and when she tilted her head upwards, Cecil found her lips and kissed her there.

"Mmm," she moaned against his mouth.

"Uhm," Emery said as she paused her steps, entering the kitchen. Her presence didn't stop Cecil from kissing his wife fully. Deciding to torture his daughter, even more, Cecil dramatically dipped Felicia and leveled her with a passionate kiss. She played right into it, lifting her leg and pointing her toes for a truly swoon worthy moment. Emery's eyes widened, and her hand found her lips covering them.

"Oh my God," she mumbled behind her fingers. "Do ya'll need a room?"

Emery spun on her heels and made a hasty retreat to the living room where the rest of the family was gathered. Hearing her pad away, both Cecil and Felicia held in a laugh as long as they could and then cracked up afterwards.

"She's never going to let us live that one down," Cecil chortled as he lifted Felicia back to standing.

It was good to laugh, and Felicia threw her head back and enjoyed the moment. Cecil saw the sparkle in her eyes, the same sparkle he saw when he fell in love with her. His heart swelled as he held her. He loved to hear her laugh.

"I don't care," Felicia chuckled. "Kiss me again, Poppy!"

# Chapter Two

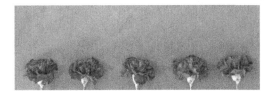

The pangs of labor intensified, and the contractions came closer together, but Kennedy hung in there. She rested the back of her head against Bryce's chest as he stood behind her, bracing her, holding her up. His warm hands caressed Kennedy's swollen belly, and they swayed from side to side to assuage her discomfort.

Doula, Joycelyn Winters quietly entered the bedroom, the sacred place where the Monroe's decided their child would be born.

"The tub is ready when you all are," she smiled. Joycelyn had been with Bryce and Kennedy since the very beginning when Ken found out she was pregnant, and the couple decided on a home birthing experience. Joycelyn had been a midwife and a doula for many years, successfully delivering more than a hundred healthy babies. The Monroe's trusted her implicitly. Joycelyn listened to what the couple wanted and their concerns. Bryce had been a little more hesitant about home birth, not because he didn't understand why Kennedy wanted it, but because he wanted to ensure she would be okay through it all. He had questions about medical attention and potential crises. That was fine with Kennedy. She would rather Bryce be assured than go into the situation with additional concerns. Joycelyn was able to answer all Bryce's questions; not with unrealistic responses but with grounded facts. That put his mind at ease, and now they were here.

"You ready for the tub, sweet," Bryce whispered in Kennedy's ear.

"Yeah," she replied. "Here comes another one."

Bryce could feel the rise and fall of Kennedy's belly. It felt like their child was doing cartwheels inside her.

"Let's go slow," Bryce encouraged, still holding her belly and bracing Kennedy as she slowly walked toward the birthing tub.

Joycelyn was right there with them. She encouraged Bryce to get in first, so he could help Kennedy get in.

"Oh, this hurts," Kennedy sighed as she sat between Bryce's legs positioning herself.

Joycelyn checked Kennedy's cervix to see how well she was progressing. Kennedy settled her head back against Bryce's shoulder and tried to relax as he gently stroked her curly tresses.

"That pressure you're feeling Kennedy is because the baby is resting down low," Joycelyn explained. "You're just about ready to push."

Bryce's eyes grew wide, and his heart started to beat

faster. Kennedy had been laboring so long, yet the idea that the baby was really on the way reawakened a host of emotions for the soon to be father.

"You ready for this, babe," He asked, pressing his cheek against hers.

The pain was so intense Kennedy couldn't even speak. All she could manage was a quick nod of the head.

"I'll go down and let the family know," Joycelyn advised. "When I get back, we can start pushing."

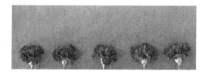

JOYCELYN DESCENDED THE STAIRS TO THE AWAITING FAMILY.

"Just wanted to let you know, Kennedy is ready to push," Joycelyn announced.

"What did she say," Felicia asked, stepping out of the kitchen and wiping her hands on the checkerboard apron she wore.

"It's time for Ken to push," Samantha iterated.

"Oh, my," Felicia sighed, instantly feeling a tightening in her own womb.

"My baby," she mused.

Samantha noticed that the checkerboard apron that her mother wiped her hands on was not twisted into a knot.

"It's gonna be fine, mom," Samantha sighed as she

wrapped her arm around her mother's shoulders. "Kennedy is going to do just fine."

Felicia leaned into her eldest daughter's arm and nodded her head. She whispered another prayer for her daughter and her soon to be grandchild. Felicia had never been more nervous than she was right now, but she had faith that God would bring them both through.

This was a new experience, not just for Felicia but also for Sam. Unlike the older Moore daughters who had the opportunity to witness the births of their siblings, Samantha was raised alone. She never had the opportunity to welcome a new member of the family. She had been the newest addition to the Moore clan. This would be wonderful and amazing to experience all together.

Cecil took over for Samantha with Felicia, who was once again fighting back the tears.

Lance watched as Samantha padded in his direction. She was wearing an interesting expression that Lance couldn't wait to ask about. He started to grin. It was a devilish grin that piqued Samantha's interest.

"What?" She brimmed as she stepped into his welcoming arms.

"I was going to ask you the same thing," Lance trilled as he pulled Samantha into his core. "The expression on your face when you walked over, I wasn't sure what that was about."

"I don't know," Samantha mused as she nuzzled against him, inhaling his enticing masculine scent.

"I know better than that," Lance countered, loving the way she felt in his arms.

He did, and Samantha knew that. There was no one who understood Samantha as Lance did. She found that both appealing and unsettling at the same time. She couldn't lie to him, nor did she intend to.

"Just thinking about family," Sam replied.

"Yeah, a new baby is a huge deal," Lance agreed. He could tell by Samantha's tone, though, that there was duality in her response. "But there's more to it, isn't it?"

"Yeah, there is," Samantha admitted. She didn't have to say more for Lance to understand where she was coming from. The notion of family, a real family, her real family was still fairly new for Samantha. There were a lot of emotions Samantha was still working through in attaching. It had been a challenge in her familial relationships as well as their relationship. Lance understood, and he was willing to ride with Samantha through whatever emotional turmoil she endured. He loved her just that much.

"Maybe one day your belly will be swollen with a baby of our own," Lance suggested, holding Sam tightly.

"You ready for that," Samantha asked, pulling back far enough to look Lance in his eyes.

"I would love to make a baby with you," Lance smiled. "Whenever you're ready."

He meant it. Sam could see the genuineness in his eyes. Having a child of her own... someone who would love her without condition had its appeal Samantha had to admit. Yet, she wasn't sure she was ready for that, not quite yet. There was so much more she wanted to accomplish, so much more she wanted to do. Although Lance provided an incredible life for her, there was still a streak of independence. She loved

Lance without question. But because she had to survive on her own for so long, Samantha never wanted to be so dependent that she couldn't take care of herself. Thankfully, Lance understood that about her. Samantha nestled back into the concave of Lance's chest and felt the beat of his heart against her flesh. He was a good man, and she would love nothing more than to give him everything his heart desired.

"But, it's still fun practicing," Lance taunted, sliding his hands from Sam's waist to the rise of her ass.

Sam's eyes widened, and she lifted herself from Lance's chest and looked around to see if anyone saw him. Playfully, she slapped at his strong arms.

"You are sooo bad," Samantha chastised, wearing a sexy smile.

"You like it, though," Lance crooned.

It's almost time," Trinity squealed, bumping her shoulder into Ivory's.

There was no response from her sister. Trinity turned fully towards Ivory and noticed she was looking off in the distance, seemingly unfocused.

"Did you hear what I said," Trinity asked, trying to get Ivory's attention.

"Huh," Ivory replied unenthusiastically.

"Where were you," Trinity pressed.

"What do you mean?"

"You were like a million miles away," Trinity replied. "Like, did you even hear what the midwife said?"

Admittedly, Ivory did not. It was true. She had been lost in her own world.

"Ken's getting ready to deliver," Trinity said. "It's almost time!"

Ivory smiled. But the smile didn't reach her eyes, and Trinity noticed.

"You look really excited," Trinity scoffed. Her sarcasm was not lost on Ivory, who watched Trinity get up from the couch and go to the other side of the room. It wasn't that Ivory wasn't happy for Kennedy. She was. And Ivory couldn't wait to be the favorite aunt and spoil her little nephew or niece. Yet, there had been so many changes in their family in what seemed like a short period of time. Not only was Kennedy married, but she was also having a baby. All of Ivory's older sisters were in significant relationships and were either married or preparing to marry. She and Trinity were the only sisters left that weren't married. But even Trinity had a man who she had just gotten off the phone smiling about. As Ivory's eyes scanned the room, she couldn't help but notice her sisters and their partners all hugged up together. Even her parents were snuggled up; dad cradling mom in his arms as she fretted about what was happening upstairs. Ivory was happy for all of them. She really was. Yet it was a stark reminder of the absence in her own life.

When Ivory felt her cellphone vibrate next to her, she rolled her eyes.

"This is my boyfriend," Ivory fussed after the cell vibrated a second time. picking it up, she swiped the screen to read the text message.

*I need you to be early to work in the morning. An important meeting has been scheduled for 10:00 a.m., and we need to prepare.*

A heavy sigh passed through Ivory's lips as she closed the screen on the phone. Every meeting was an important meeting. *It's always something;* Ivory thought as she put the phone on the couch face down. As an international attaché for Sudanese Diplomat, Fazila Adebisi, Ivory spent a lot of time in important meetings with high-powered individuals. And with Diplomat Adebisi's focus on the plight of the young girls in her home country, those meetings had become even more frequent and even more critical. Ivory loved the work. She felt as though it was purposed, and she was doing something important that could really make a difference in the lives of some of the world's most vulnerable individuals. Still, her work kept her busy, sometimes to the exclusion of being able to spend time with family, and certainly to the exclusion of being in a real relationship. And although Ivory found herself in the room with some of the most influential international men in the world, she was all about business when she was working. Hooking up at work was not an option, and not one Ivory entertained even though some of the men she encountered were very impressive. She just didn't have time. Work dominated her life.

Ivory shook her head. Even when the call came that Kennedy was in labor, Ivory was just leaving a late afternoon meeting. She hadn't even had time to go home and change clothes. But she was glad to be here with the family. She wouldn't miss the birth of this new baby for anything. Ivory sighed again. There was no point in getting all sentimental about the lack of love in her life. This time was not about her. Shaking off her personal funk, Ivory got up from the couch, determined to focus on something, and someone other than herself.

# Chapter Three

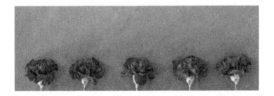

"Uhhhhh," Kennedy groaned. The burning sensation she felt in her core hurt like hell.

"You got this, babe," Bryce encouraged as he helped Kennedy hold her knees back. "You got this."

"Okay, Kennedy," Joycelyn began, "with the next contraction, I need you to push."

"I'm so tired," Kennedy cried. "I can't." She wanted an all-natural birth, so there were no meds to take the edge off. Kennedy was hurting, but she wouldn't have it any other way. Still, the bear was unbearable.

"Yes, you can," Bryce insisted. He stroked Kennedy's brow and then gently trailed the side of her face until he titled her chin and waited until their eyes met.

"I have so much faith in you," he reminded Kennedy. He could see her struggling. He hurt for her. But Bryce knew what Kennedy wanted, what she insisted on from the time they found out they were pregnant. Compromise at this point was not an option. No matter the pain, Kennedy wouldn't want that.

"Come on, babe," Bryce crooned. "We're almost there. You're doing so great. Just a little bit more."

She could be mad with Bryce so easily right now. She could blame him for what she was going through and lash out because he put her in this predicament. But Ken didn't have the energy for it. She barely had the energy to breathe.

"This baby is stubborn like you," Ken fussed as another pang started to crest.

Bryce chuckled. "My stubborn ass loves you, though," Bryce lovingly clapped back.

"You better," Ken groaned.

"Oh, my God!"

"That's right, Kennedy, breathe with it, and push!" Joycelyn said.

"You got this, sweet, push!"

Kennedy closed her eyes and did her best to block out the pain she felt. All she wanted to do was see her baby, and she had to push through the pain to do that. Bearing down, Kennedy pushed with everything she had.

"AAAAAAHHHHH!!!!!"

She cried out so loud that all movement stopped on the lower level as Kennedy's piercing groan traveled through the floor.

Felicia grabbed Cecil's hand and squeezed. "My baby," she grimaced.

"Bryce, if you look over, you can see the baby's head," Joycelyn continued.

Slowly, Bryce did what Joycelyn suggested, and his mouth fell open at the sight.

"Wow," Bryce gasped. "Wow, sweet." Bryce's eyes blinked rapidly as they began to mist over with tears. "Our baby is right there."

Kennedy's heart swelled. Bryce was already in love, and she knew firsthand what it felt like to be loved by him. When Bryce leaned back and planted a warm kiss on Kennedy's cheek, she could tell he was fighting back tears.

"Kennedy, I need you to push one more time," Joycelyn continued after clearing the baby's passageways. "Breathe with her, Bryce."

"Come on, sweet, one more time."

He started their breathing pattern, the one they practiced in Lamaze. "He hee hoo. He hee hoo."

Kennedy fell in sync. "He hee hoo. He hee hoo."

Kennedy's breathing pattern stopped short as a stabbing pang struck deep.

"Oh my God, oh my God, oh my God!!"

"Mmhmm, come on, Kennedy, push through it."

Joycelyn helped as much as she could, to help ease the baby's shoulders out of the birthing canal. Kennedy panted. It was hard to catch her breath as everything hurt.

"One more big push, Kennedy. You got this! You can do it!" Joycelyn encouraged.

A growl poured from Kennedy as she dug deep for the last bit of strength she had. The burning sensation was so intense.

"That's right, mom," Joycelyn smiled. "Now, lift your baby to you."

Kennedy watched as her precious gift of life eased from her body. With both hands, Ken reached down and lifted their child the rest of the way and then turned the baby to her.

"It's a boy," Joycelyn sighed. Gently, she patted the baby's bottom as Kennedy laid the child on her chest.

"It's a boy," Kennedy repeated as tears poured down her flushed cheeks. "Babe, you have a son."

They were both overjoyed and rendered speechless. And when their son cried for the first time, tears of joy fell from both his parent's eyes.

Bryce couldn't speak. He had a son. Kennedy had given him a son. Words could not express just how overjoyed he was. And when he looked down and saw his son, Bryce couldn't believe it even though he witnessed it himself. He was a dad.

KENNEDY AND HER NEWLY EXPANDED FAMILY SPENT SOME TIME together after Bryce cut the umbilical cord, and Kennedy had a chance to get settled in the bed with their new son in her arms. The doula went downstairs and invited the family up.

"They are ready for you," she announced.

"All of us?" Emery asked as she looked around the room.

"That's what the new parents said," the doula confirmed.

Emery looked towards her parents, seeking confirmation that they all should go. The rest of the Moore sisters turned, almost in unison to see what their mother had to say. Felicia smiled as tears spilled onto her cheeks and nodded her affirmation. She couldn't stop crying. Felicia was just so overjoyed. She reached out, and Cecil grabbed her hand, escorting his beloved wife behind the doula up the stairs to see their grandchild. Bryce's parents and the rest of the family followed closely behind.

"This is so exciting," Trinity smiled, wrapping her arm around Ivory's as the sisters mounted the stairs.

It was exciting as they all piled into the expansive master bedroom. Bryce waited until everyone was there before making his announcement. There were already tears in many of the family members' eyes, even before Bryce spoke, sitting next to his wife on the bed. Just seeing Kennedy glowing holding her son, and the importance of the moment was heartwarming for everyone.

"Family, meet our son, Cecil Bryce Monroe."

Hearing his son's name, even as he spoke it, choked Bryce up, but he pushed through, not wanting to break down in front of everybody. The grandmas were the first to approach the bed, oohing and aahing over their new grandson.

"He's just so handsome," Felicia cooed as Kennedy placed the baby in her mother's arms. Mrs. Monroe held him next, and she cried, as well; overjoyed that her son was blessed with a son of his own.

"If he is anything like you, Bryce, you will never be disappointed," his mom said, as Bryce hugged her around the waist. Cecil was stunned. He had no idea Kennedy intended to name her child after him. As their eyes met, Cecil mouthed a thank you to his daughter as they both beamed with pride.

"There is no greater gift anyone has ever given me," He whispered in Kennedy's ear after padding over and kissing her lightly on the forehead. Cecil didn't reserve his happiness to just Kennedy. He walked over to Bryce, and as his son-in-law stood up to greet him, Cecil pulled Bryce int a warm hug.

"Thank you, son."

"My pleasure," Bryce replied. "We wouldn't have it any other way."

It was hard for the Moore girls to wait their turn to greet their nephew. It was getting late. Ivory had a meeting first thing in the morning, but there was no way she was leaving before getting to hold Cecil. Just then, Ivory's phone buzzed again.

"Ugh!!!" She exhaled loudly, drawing the ire of Trinity.

"I know that is not your job bugging you again," Trinity said, shaking her head.

"It never stops," Ivory complained, reaching into her pocket and swiping the screen. It was another message from her boss.

**The VIP's we're meeting with tomorrow need to have the meeting moved up two hours. Scheduling conflict. I need you here by 6 a.m. so we can be prepared for the meeting at 8.**

*Dammit*, Ivory bemoaned. It was a good thing she loved

her job. The work they were doing was so important. That made the long days and nights worth it. Still, a six-a.m. call time was brutal, considering it was already close to midnight. Ivory felt a tug on her arm.

"It's our turn," Samantha said, smiling at her younger sister. Immediately, Ivory forgot all about her job woes as she padded alongside the rest of her sisters towards Kennedy and the baby.

"Hey, sis," Daphne crooned, leaning over and hugging Kennedy.

"Hey," Kennedy smiled.

"You look so beautiful, all glowing and shit," Daphne whispered so her parents wouldn't hear her curse.

"Thank you, girl," Kennedy smized with her mouth and her eyes simultaneously.

"It's true; Felicity agreed as the girls piled on the huge bed, just like they did when they were younger.

"Inspired to have one of your own?" Kennedy teased. Felicity and her beau Garrett had been hot and heavy for nearly a year.

"Chile, please," Felicity clapped back. "I already have to fight Garrett off, with his young, fine ass. If I tell him I want a baby, he'll make that thang happen quick, fast, and in a hurry!"

"Either Emery or Sam will be next," Ivory mused.

"Why do you say that?" Emery questioned.

"Cause," Ivory replied. "You two are the oldest."

"Did she just call us old," Samantha asked.

"I think so," Emery agreed.

"Well," Aubrey chimed. "If the shoe fits."

"Ken and Bryce just couldn't keep their hands off each other, apparently," Trinity taunted. "Messing up the order and stuff!"

"Whatever," Kennedy quipped. "Do ya'll want to see your nephew or not?"

"Of course," Charity piped up. "If mom and dad give him up!"

"Girl, we might be waiting," Ivory taunted.

"Just hold on a minute," Felicia fussed, turning towards her daughters. "Just one more kiss from Nana."

Felicia was in love and in awe. She kissed Cecil lightly on the brim of his baby blue hat and reluctantly handed him over to his mom.

"I want him back," Felicia warned.

As the sisters saw their nephew for the first time, there was a collective sigh.

"Awwwww."

Felicia wasn't the only one instantly in love.

"Cecil, meet your aunties," Kennedy cooed.

There was a swoon that moved throughout the sisters.

"He is beautiful," Felicity smiled.

"And look at those curls," Daphne added as she gently adjusted the baby's hat.

All the aunties took turns holding their nephew. Ivory was nervous about holding him.

"He's so little," she mused as Kennedy sat Cecil safely in Ivory's arms. But it didn't take long for Ivory's nerves to settle. And when Cecil wrapped his tiny fingers around Ivory's, her heart melted. "Amazing."

Ivory felt hot tears pressing against her eyes as she held

her nephew. He represented so much, not just to his parents but to the entire family. He represented the manifestation of what real love looked like, as well as the beginning of a new generation. Ivory was completely moved. She was just as reluctant as her mother was to have to give him away.

"I want to be first on the list for babysitting detail," Ivory clamored as she handed Cecil off to Daphne.

"Uh no ma'am," Trinity chimed. "If I'm not mistaken, my babysitting coupon from the shower trumps all verbal requests."

"Ya'll is a mess," Samantha laughed.

"How much longer before I get my grandson back," Felicia countered, sliding her hand up her hip and resting it there.

Her commentary made everyone laugh.

Charity leaned over to Kennedy and whispered in her ear. "Honey, ya'll ain't gone never get rid of her," Charity laughed. "Mom and dad just might move in."

Kennedy laughed even though it hurt a little. "That'll be fine with me," Ken smiled. "Built in babysitters, girl."

"Built in birth control," Trinity cackled.

"I might need it," Kennedy chuckled. "At least for the next six weeks."

"Yeah, you better be careful," Sam added. "Ya'll will be having number two before you know it."

"You hear that Bryce," Aubrey called out to Bryce, who wasn't too far away. "Back away."

Bryce smiled and winked at Kennedy.

"Girl, you are in trouble!" Ivory hummed.

"I know," Kennedy agreed."

Although she was having a great time, Ivory felt compelled to check her watch. It was well after one o'clock in the morning. She had to be at a mandatory meeting in just a few hours.

"I hate to break up the party, but I have to go," Ivory sighed.

"I hate your job," Kennedy fussed her lips turned down into a frown.

"We all hate your job," Felicity agreed.

"We all can't own our own restaurant, Ken," Ivory replied.

"Don't make Ivory feel bad," Emery interjected. "She's doing good stuff."

"Thank you, Em," Ivory smiled as she eased off the bed. She padded over to where her parents were standing and gave each of them a hug.

"Call us when you get home, okay," Cecil instructed.

"Yes sir," Ivory said, accepting a kiss to the cheek from her dad.

"Promise?" Felicia added.

"I will," Ivory agreed.

As Ivory separated from her parents, she took one last glance over her shoulder, seeing her sisters enjoying each other and the new baby. She padded out of the room and down the stairs. By the time Ivory was in her car, she was already missing her family.

# Chapter Four

"*M*r. West, we should be arriving at our destination in just a few minutes," the driver advised.

This wasn't Roman's regular driver. The formality of the conversation between the two suggested that. The conversation between Roman and his regular driver was much more relaxed because of how long they'd been together. Roman only intended to be in Atlanta long enough for the meeting and then fly out immediately after. He didn't begrudge the importance of the meeting. The emergent nature made it critical. He just hoped that those involved could focus on the business at hand and not prolong it with conundrums and emotionality that would only serve to inflame the sensitive nature, typically without resolution. Roman hated to waste time, regardless of how important the context was.

It didn't take long for the driver to turn the Bentley onto the paved private drive of the Senegalese Embassy. The drive was lined with big men in dark suits and mirrored sunglasses that shielded their eyes from the sun and prevented anyone from determining just where they were looking. The driver parked the car and came around the back, opening the door for his distinguished passenger. Roman slid his Cartier Panthere sunglasses onto his mocha face and adjusted them on the bridge of his perfectly balanced nose before stepping out of the Bentley parked in front of the entryway. Roman's measured strides that carried his six-foot-two frame always drew attention. Whether it was the low click of his Salvatore Ferragamo crocodile skin loafers or how the custom steel gray suit hung from his masculine body in just the right way, or how the crisp white shirt that fell smoothly against his pecs accentuated the dark chocolate of his skin, Roman's presence always drew attention. And that attention intensified as the ornate doors of the embassy were opened for him, and Roman strode down the high polished marble floors that led to the meeting space.

Ivory was rushing. It was just a few minutes before the meeting was slated to start, and she had just been given a last-minute instruction to run to the other side of the building to retrieve some additional information. Last night, Ivory had been so wired from the birth of her nephew that it was difficult for Ivory to sleep once she got home. She tossed and turned with flashes of all things love that played across her mind; the intimate kisses shared between partners, the hand holding that just seemed so natural, the stolen glances that nobody else was supposed to see, culminating in the outpouring of love that was physically felt when they were introduced to their newest family member. The theme was the same. It was all love, which was great, except Ivory found herself on the outside looking in. And that is the part that kept her tossing and turning for most of the night. She was the one waiting to have her hand held. She was the one waiting for that stolen look that meant so much between two people that loved each other. Ivory was inserted into those moments, whether she was dreaming or reminiscing. But when she turned to see the person who was hers and hers alone, there was no one there. Ivory couldn't even manage to supplant a past boyfriend into that space. It was sad, really. So, she didn't sleep well. She almost overslept after slapping the clock a few times, traffic was horrific as usual, and the whole morning had been one big rush.

"Ugh," Ivory grumbled internally, as she tried to navigate through the plethora of people moving through the main corridors of the embassy. She had to wear a smile, given her position. But that didn't stop her from being mildly irritated from having to tiptoe and pivot, so she didn't run into anyone.

"Excuse me. Sorry. Excuse me," Ivory repeated on a loop as she moved through; her three-inch sensible shoes clicking decisively against the marble floors.

Maybe it was the hum of her alto voice that caught Roman's attention, or maybe it was the rhythmic click of her heels that inclined him to her swift movement.

"Sorry," she uttered, moving past Roman leaving him with only a fleeting glance and a whiff of her feminine scent. His eyes trailed her form as she continued down the long hallway. The flounce of her striking red hair and the swerve of her full hips entranced Roman as he found himself moving in the same direction she was. Her movement down the hall, threading through the people was like an effortless dance. Roman didn't realize that the pace of his own strides increased as he continued to be enchanted by her alluring movements; the black pencil skirt she wore hugging her shapely curves and taut waist. Roman drew closer to her as they continued to move in the same direction.

And then she was gone in an instant, behind some door that read private. Roman briefly paused, looking at the door she disappeared behind, a part of him hoping she would reappear.

"Excuse me."

A different voice and a slight bump from behind drew Roman away from his wayward gaze. He had no choice but to keep moving forward. It was almost time for the meeting, and Roman disliked tardiness, even from himself. Finally, arriving at the designated space for the meeting, Roman entered the well-appointed space. Several of the dignitaries at the table, Roman immediately recognized. It was important in his business to know who the movers and shakers were. Undoubtedly, many of those in the room knew who Roman West was. Although he wasn't a diplomat, Mr. West was frequently invited to international meetings of this magnitude because of his philanthropic efforts and his multimillion-dollar international finance business. After shaking a few hands, Roman took his seat at the circular table. There were two rows of chairs; the first row for the dignitaries with microphones positioned immediately in front of them and the second for their translators and attaches. There were also name plates for each of the special guests, so it was clear who was there, and when the time came, who was speaking. Roman adjusted his lengthy frame in the seat and casually glanced around the room before focusing his attention on the folder that was placed in front of each seat. While Roman perused the material and continued to acknowledge dignitaries that continued to recognize him, he thought back to the vision he saw in the hallway just a few moments before. A slight smile eased across his lips; one he diminished quickly as a few of the female onlookers began to notice.

The sound of fast-moving clicks could be heard down the marble hall once again. Ivory was rushing. The meeting was just about to start, and she wasn't in position. By now, Ivory should have been sitting to the six of Diplomat Fazilah Adebisi. Fazilah hand selected Ivory because she was fluent in Dinka and Arabic, both oral and written; the native languages of Fazilah's home country. And although Diplomat Adebisi had been in the United States for several years, she felt comfortable speaking natively although she was proficient in English. Speaking with Ivory was easy. Ivory understood Fazilah no matter what language she chose to speak.

As Ivory opened the door to the meeting space, she heard the moderator calling the meeting to order. Ivory was so tempted to throw up the Missionary Baptist finger, excusing herself from being tardy, but she resisted the urge. On her tiptoes, Ivory hustled to her seat, doing her best to be invisible.

But Ivory wasn't invisible. Roman saw her as soon as she entered the space. Maybe it was her beautifully brilliant red afro that drew his eye, or maybe it was the incredible impression embedded in his mind of the sexy swivel of her hips. Whatever it was, Roman's eyes trailed the mystery woman until she sat down on the second row. The words the moderator said ceased to be important as he couldn't take his eyes off her.

"Diplomat Adebisi," the moderator announced. "The floor is yours."

Although the diplomat was beautiful in her own right, donning traditional garb and headdress representative of her homeland, Roman barely noticed her. But having the diplomat take the floor gave him an excuse to look in her direction, although his focus was on the woman behind her. But she was so busy working, her head hadn't come up so Roman could clearly see her face.

"The conditions that our girls, our daughters continue to face, is more than tragic," Adebisi said. "It is heart-wrenching to anyone who has a heart."

That comment did cause Ivory to lift her head, nodding in support of what Fazilah had to say. And the sarcasm was not lost on anyone in the room. Fazilah waged war against many of those in power, both in Sudan and in other countries, who failed to appropriately respond to the conditions in her country. They reacted heartlessly, and she wouldn't let them forget it.

"Can you imagine a nine- year-old little girl, not just any nine-year-old, a nine-year-old child that you know. Now imagine that she is in tears because she is being forced to marry a man five times her age. She doesn't know this man, and she doesn't have a choice. She's crying, not just because she's being torn from the only family she's ever known and being snatched away by a stranger. But this little girl is crying because all she really wants to do is go to school, play with dolls, jump rope, be with her friends. She wants to be a child."

Fazilah paused for dramatic effect to allow the scenario to play out in the minds of the power-players around her.

"Now, imagine that little girl is twelve now. And, she gets pregnant. Her body is barely capable of such a thing, but it happens. There's no shame, right, because she is married. But she is still a little girl, desiring to go to school and play with dolls and be with her friends."

The room was silent. There were no sidebars or impolite conversations. Everyone was mesmerized by what Adebisi had to say. Some even knew it to be a reality in their own countries. Still, hearing it spoken out loud, reminded everyone of the travesties some must endure by no fault of their own.

"Stay with me because this little girl's story is almost done," Fazilah continued. "She struggles to hold the child in her child-sized womb. The little girl doesn't want to be a mommy. She still misses her own. She doesn't want to be married. The man that occupies her marital bed is still a stranger and a brute. She doesn't want any part of what is happening to her. But what choice does she have."

Fazilah's voice cracked as she recalled the story. Hearing that break in her solemn delivery was an emotional jolt. Ivory leaned in, placing a gentle hand to Fazilah's shoulder, hoping to give her enough strength to continue.

"When the little girls' water breaks, she is home alone.

She doesn't know what to do, and she is frightened out of her mind. The pains are coming hard, and she feels movement inside her that seems foreign in as much as it is painful. There's a problem. She can't fix it. The little girl doesn't know what to do. The umbilical cord is choking off the baby's oxygen supply. She's scared, and her teary eyes are wide, seeing all the blood and fluids pouring from her small frame. She can't believe that a person is coming from her body. Still, she doesn't know what to do.

Fazilah pauses again as she fights back tears of her own. No matter how many times she's told the story, the truth of it still hurts deeply. Fazilah took a deep, slow breath and pressed forward, despite the pain.

"Unfortunately, the baby doesn't make it. However, instead of being offered counseling and condolences, the little girl is charged with infanticide and sentenced to prison. Prison, can you imagine? Interestingly enough, the little girl is not as sad as people would think. Prison means no husband to assault her frail young body at night, possibly impregnating her with another child. She manages not to be sad about being incarcerated for a crime she did not commit. How can I say that you might ask? I say it with the greatest conviction. The crimes were committed against the little girl. She was a child bride, forcibly impregnated. She was a child who had a complicated birth she couldn't manage. She was charged with murder for a child that nearly killed her."

Fazilah paused and looked around the room, searching the eyes and faces of the dignitaries around her. It was only when she knew she had everyone's full attention did Fazilah finish the story.

"If it wasn't for someone who learned about that little girl's story and fought like hell to have her released, I wouldn't be sitting here with you today."

Fazilah watched as the shock and awe began to resonate on the faces of the people around her.

"Yes, I am that little girl."

Ivory's eyes misted over, and she lowered her head, trying to keep anyone from seeing her crying. But her eyes weren't the only ones filled with tears. Many around the room also lowered their heads as they attempted to pull themselves together behind the diplomat's heart-crushing revelation. He noticed, though. He noticed everything about her; the tilt of her head when she was attentive, the slant of her nose perfectly balanced against the fullness of her lips, the elegance of her neck, and the caramel mocha of her skin. *Nah,* he thought to himself as he examined her face as discriminately as possible. *Couldn't* be, he mused as his heart started to beat a little faster. And then Roman noticed something more. He thought the woman sitting behind the diplomat looked familiar. Roman's head tilted slightly as he realized who that woman was - his junior high school crush. With recognition came a familiar feeling in his gut. The smile that was previously dancing on the corners of his lips returned in earnest as memories of the girl he loved from afar sat right in front of him. It was her, wasn't it? Roman needed one more chance to see if it was really Ivory, his Ivory. He hoped he would get the chance.

"I know it's hard to believe," Diplomat Adebisi went on, "but I am here because someone thought enough of me, enough of my situation to fight for me. They fought, not only with their words but with their wallets. Child brides and infanticide have plagued Sudan, especially South Sudan, for many years. That doesn't make it right. History makes it acceptable to the masses and forgotten by far too many. There are those in this room who are aware of the plight of young girls in my country, and unfortunately, many other countries where their voices aren't heard because they are too afraid to speak against history and patriarchy and abuse. All I need is one," Fazilah iterated. "All I need is one person in this room who is willing to fight alongside me. Will you be that one?"

As hard as it had been for Roman to focus once he thought he saw someone familiar, it grew even more difficult once the meeting was adjourned. It wasn't that Roman was insensitive to Diplomat Adebisi's plea nor that he wasn't concerned for the plight of the young women in her country. He was very concerned and moved. Still, flashes of stolen moments when he saw Ivory walking down the halls at school when she didn't even know he existed consumed his thoughts. Roman had to know if it was really her. As he stood to his full height, Roman's eyes scanned the room to try and find her.

"Bonjour."

Roman felt a cool hand pressed against his wrist. His eyes were still roving over the space to try and find Ivory. Then, she stepped in front of him, compelling his attention to follow.

"Bonjour Monsieur West," she insisted, doing her best to capture Roman's full attention.

"Bonjour," Roman replied to avoid the presumption of

rudeness. It was the Diplomat from France, Amelie Bissett. Roman had met Amelie a time or two. She was forthright in expressing her interest in him, but Roman didn't feel the same. He did manage a slight smile as his gaze returned to searching for Ivory. Amelie was not easily dissuaded as she managed to wrap both her hands around his wrist as she continued.

"Weren't you absolutely moved by the madame's story?" Amelie stepped even closer to Roman, eliminating nearly all his personal space.

"Yes, it was compelling," Roman replied as he took a polite yet noticeable step back. *Where is she*, he thought. And then, he saw her, just a passing glance, but he found her amongst the gatherings in the room.

"Excuse me," Roman offered as he reclaimed his wrist and his space. Before the French Diplomat could voice an objection, Roman's long strides took him across the room. He was headed directly for Ivory. She was the only thing he was thinking about. He had to know if it was really her. Roman sidestepped a few people, offering a polite smile as he moved. And then his inner voice started to raise questions; those he hadn't considered as he had been so singularly focused. What if it wasn't the real Ivory? What if she didn't remember him, or worst yet, remember him as fondly as he remembered her? His pace slowed slightly in response to the queries racing through his head. Roman would hate to be all excited only to be let down in the end.

As the group parted, Roman got his first clear visual of the woman he hoped was Ivory. She was mesmerizing, even more now than she had been in his youth. She was standing next to Diplomat Adebisi, and the two were entertaining a congresswoman from the US. Roman had no choice but to hang back. For the first time in his pursuit of her, Roman felt awkward, standing there trying to look occupied. This was one time he wished someone would approach him with a conversation, any conversation, despite how irrelevant. No one did, and Roman did his best to blend. Sliding his hands into his pockets, Roman didn't resist the urge to look in the diplomat's direction. Looking at the diplomat brought 'her' into view.

She was still stunning, and trying not to stare at her became increasingly difficult. And then it happened. Their eyes met across the crowded room. Roman didn't even realize that his breath stopped short in his chest when contact was made. He dared not look away. But, what if she didn't see him as he saw her? What if he was wrong, and it wasn't Ivory? The thump in his chest could be felt in his throat as time absolutely stood still. Ivory's eyes widened, and she leaned slightly forward, trying to clarify who she saw. Her mouth parted slightly, and her brow furrowed. *That couldn't be, could it*, Ivory thought to herself. Roman waited with bated breath, hoping against hope that his inclinations were right. Then, she smiled. She saw him.

The swell of Roman's heart was palatable, and he inhaled a breath he didn't even know he needed. It was Ivory; his Ivory, and she remembered him.

Ivory couldn't believe it. *Roman? From junior high school, Roman? What in the world was he doing here?* After seeing and recognizing a blast from the past, Ivory found it difficult to focus on the task at hand. She had been translating in multiple languages between the guests and the diplomat as they approached. But now, Ivory found herself tongue-tied, and she couldn't take her eyes off him. Roman was not the friend-guy she used to know. His face was the same, more mature, of course, but enough for recognition to take place. But as Ivory tried to focus on the task at hand, her eyes continued to trail back to him. Nothing else about the Roman she knew was the same, in a good way... a damn good way.

She felt his eyes on her as heat rose to her cheeks while a juxtaposed chill trickled down her spine. That had never happened to her before, not with Roman. She smiled again as a laugh erupted in her spirit. She had to contain it because of where she was, yet Ivory certainly felt it. She knew he was in the room and now she couldn't unknow it. Roman started to move, in Ivory's direction, no less. Her heart leapt in her chest, and she felt a huge surge or nervous energy course through her. Why though? Little Roman from back in the day shouldn't have her feeling some kind of way, but dammit he did.

Ivory parted her full lips and blew out slowly, trying to calm the butterflies that ravaged her insides.

"Are you alright," Diplomat Adebisi asked, noticing that Ivory was a little slow with the translation.

Flushing with embarrassment, Ivory cleared her throat and willed herself to focus on the matter at hand. But then, in her periphery, Ivory saw movement. Slowly, as she lifted her head, Ivory's flesh heated again, and a smile teased the corners of her lips as she saw Roman strolling in her direction. She felt compelled to place her hand on her chest as she felt her heart thundering underneath her fingertips. *Why the hell is my heart beating so fast*, Ivory questioned; shifting her weight from one foot to the other. She couldn't keep still, stop grinning, or quiet the banging of her heart. And the butterflies? Oh, baby! They were doing back flips and somersaults in her belly. Ivory's face was so warm, and her grin was so uncontrollable, she couldn't even look at Roman as he neared.

"Mr. West," Diplomat Adebisi sang. "So nice to see you once again."

"And you as well," Roman replied. Like a gentleman, he accepted the gracefully extended hand from the diplomat. Although he had the diplomat's full attention, Roman struggled being so close to Ivory, especially since she still wouldn't look in his direction. He wanted to engage her beautiful brown eyes up close and personal - final confirmation of who she was. Even without that, though, being so close to her, Roman knew it in his heart, in his soul, in his spirit that the mystery woman was Ivory Moore. They both swooned, unbeknownst to the other; Roman's swoon was connected to the past. Ivory's was grounded in the present.

"I was moved by your story and would like to make a donation," Roman offered.

"Ah, that warms my heart, Mr. West," Fazilah smiled. "Anything you can do would be greatly appreciated.

Ivory did her best, continuing to entertain the other VIP's waiting to speak with the diplomat. Roman reached inside the jacket of his tailored suit and pulled out his Italian leather covered check book. He already planned to make a donation; therefore, most of the check was complete. But hearing the plight of the young women in Sudan pricked Roman's heart. After a few seconds, he handed the check to Fazilah.

"Thank y-."

Fazilah's words stopped short. Her eyes dropped down to her hand and then back to Roman. Ivory was pulled into their exchange when she felt a tight grip on her wrist. Fazilah reached out for Ivory, completely overwhelmed by Roman's generosity.

"Are you sure?" Fazilah stammered. Ivory looked at her boss who's mouth remained slightly ajar, and then Ivory peeked at the check. Now her mouth was slightly ajar as well. "A million dollars," Fazilah cried, her eyes filled with tears.

"It's the least I can do," Roman replied. "And if there is anything I can do, please do not hesitate to contact me. Roman's eyes traveled to Ivory. This time, she was looking at him, and their eyes met again. The gasp on Ivory's lips slowly faded as she felt Roman drink her in fully. Thankfully, Fazilah was too busy trying to recover from the generous donation he made to notice the VIP and her attaché having a moment. And it was a moment, one that weakened Ivory's knees.

This time when he reached in his jacket pocket, it was to pull out a business card that listed both his business and personal number. The card he gladly handed to Ivory. Roman didn't let go immediately as their hands inadvertently made contact. There was a rush of energy that engulfed them both. It was electric. The natural inclination was to pull away from the shock of it all, but neither did.

Roman knew he couldn't hold up the line too much longer. Still, he wasn't ready to leave Ivory's presence. But he had too. Those behind Roman were getting restless. Those closest enjoyed the exchange.

"Thank you again, Mr. West," Fazilah sighed as he started to walk away. "We can't thank you enough."

"My pleasure," Roman crooned as his eyes slowly trailed from Ivory to the diplomat. They parted, but not before Roman looked over his shoulder and smiled for her.

# Chapter Five

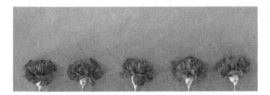

There were still people in line who wanted an opportunity to speak to Diplomat Adebisi. Some wanted to share how moved they were by her story, while others wanted to extend assistance in one way or the other. Ivory had a job to do. She had to be there with Fazilah until the last guest greeted her. It was a struggle. She couldn't stop thinking about him. Ivory was still stunned at the coincidence. Although she loved her job, she begrudged having to leave her family the night before so she could make it on time. She would have loved to hold her new nephew one more time and just enjoy the people she loved the most. Now though, after running into Roman, maybe being at work wasn't so bad?

But she watched as he walked away until she couldn't see him any longer. Ivory wondered if he extended the business card to her so she would call, or was it really for the diplomat? *Nah*, Ivory thought. Something in the way Roman smiled at her suggested he intended the card for her. As she continued assisting Diplomat Adebisi with the last few guests, Ivory kind of regretted not having the chance to catch up with him.

"I still can't believe the incredible generosity of Mr. West. Can you?" Fazilah asked as she and Ivory exited the meeting space.

"No, I can't," Ivory replied as they entered the hallway. "What exactly does Mr. West do," Ivory inquired, "to be able to give so much?"

"All I know is that he is a successful businessman," Fazilah answered.

They walked a few more paces until they reached the diplomat's office.

"You've worked hard today, Ivory. Go home or, better yet, go do something fun. I can handle the rest."

"Are you sure?" Ivory asked.

"Of course," Fazilah replied. "Thanks for everything, and I will see you Monday morning at nine o'clock sharp."

"Thanks, see you then."

"Oh, and hug that new nephew for me," Fazilah called after.

"I will," Ivory smiled.

The only sound that could be heard was Ivory's heels clicking rhythmically as she moved towards the exit of the embassy. Although Ivory was a bit tired from the day, it was still early. She could go back to Kennedy's house and see Baby Cecil. That put a smile on her face as she pushed open the exit door and stepped into the warm afternoon air. Reaching in her purse, Ivory pulled out her sunglasses and her cell phone. She slid the glasses on her face to shield her eyes from the brightness of the sun and unlocked her phone. Although Kennedy would never say she couldn't come, Ivory wanted to be courteous and make sure it was a good time. Ken had just pushed out a whole human. She could very well be tired and resting. Ivory wouldn't want to disturb that. She dialed the number and put the phone up to her ear. Ivory looked around, trying to remember where she parked her car.

Then, she froze in place, and with a smirk and a slight shake of her head, Ivory ended the call before the first ring. A feeling that was becoming all too familiar washed over Ivory as she saw Roman leaning against a stretch limousine parked right in front of the building. Ivory had been so busy rummaging through her purse, she hadn't taken time to look up until that very moment.

"You didn't think I was going to let you get away that easily, did you," Roman crooned as he strolled in Ivory's direction.

*Damn!* She was glad he didn't, but Ivory didn't say that. Instead, she took a moment to take him in fully, from head to toe. This was not the same Roman from back in the day. His tall, muscular frame couldn't be hidden by the custom-fit suit that draped his form.

When Roman reached her, his heart thundered in his chest. He stopped just short, feeling her aura and doing his best to contain his excitement in seeing her once again.

"Ms. Moore," he chortled.

"Mr. West," she grinned, looking up into his deep brown eyes.

Roman reached down and wrapped his strong arms around Ivory's taut waist and pulled her into him. She was literally lifted by his strength onto her tiptoes as she laced her arms around his thickly corded neck. Ivory melded into him, inhaling his enticing masculine scent and feeling the strength of his core pressed against her. For Roman, hugging Ivory, having her in his arms was the fulfillment of a fantasy, a dream he had a long time ago that finally came to fruition. It goes without saying that he didn't want to let her go. She immediately felt right in his arms. It was more than Roman ever imagined it could be.

It would be easy to stay there, nestled so snugly to him. Yet, Ivory knew she needed to pull away, just a little. She knew him before when they were much younger. She knew nothing about him now.

As Ivory eased back, putting some distance between her body and his, she once again looked up into his oh too handsome face.

"I can't believe it's really you," he crooned.

"Who would have thought," Ivory said, taking a step back and allowing Roman's arms to fall from around her.

She started to chuckle, and Roman was intrigued.

"What?" He asked, looking at her curiously. All the while, a smoldering smile remained on his perfect lips.

"It's just so weird looking up at you," Ivory grinned. "You are certainly not the little Romy Rom from back in the day!" She remembered having to look down at him in junior high. He was at least two inches shorter than she was.

Roman had to laugh. He hadn't heard that nickname in years.

"Nah," he smiled. "I grew up, and so did you."

There was something about the way he said it that flushed Ivory's cheeks. Casually, she ran her manicured fingers through her loosely coiled tresses and turned slightly away so Roman couldn't see the inerasable smile that danced on her lips. He saw her, though. What Ivory didn't know is that he felt much the same way. She had been his secret crush for as long as he'd known her. Growing up and time separated them, with both graduating and pursuing different journeys. Still, that feeling seeing Ivory took Roman back to how he felt seemingly a lifetime ago.

"So," Ivory began, desperately trying to regain control of her flighty emotions. "What has been going on with you?"

"I could ask the same thing," Roman echoed.

"True, true," Ivory replied.

"What are you about to do now?"

She thought about the phone call she made and then looked at Roman again.

"I didn't have a whole lot planned," Ivory answered. "I'm sure you have something on your agenda, though," she surmised as the driver waited patiently in the luxury vehicle.

"You are my agenda," Roman crooned. "That is, if you want to be."

"Still as smooth as ever," Ivory chuckled.

"Well, some things haven't changed," Roman smiled. "Come with me. Let's have a late lunch and catch up."

Roman waited for Ivory's reply. She wanted to go, but Ivory didn't want to seem too anxious. When Roman put his hands together as though he was praying, Ivory laughed. He looked so sweet and innocent.

"Let's do lunch," she smiled.

"Excellent," Roman smiled as well. "After you."

Like the gentleman he was, Roman extended his hand, guiding Ivory in the direction of the awaiting vehicle. She felt his firm hand pressed gently against the center of her back. His touch felt natural and right in a weird kind of way.

*Don't overthink it,* Ivory heard her inner voice caution. There was a part of Ivory that wanted to ignore the subconscious warning completely. But she wouldn't. Ivory knew better than that. There were times when she didn't listen and regretted it. That was history she didn't want to repeat.

"Good afternoon, ma'am," the driver said as he opened the back door.

"Good afternoon."

Roman was right there, taking over for the driver to ensure Ivory got safely in the vehicle and slid in beside her once Ivory was settled. The driver closed the door and rounded the back of the vehicle.

"It's been a while since I've been in Atlanta," Roman said. "Any recommendations?"

"Hmmm," Ivory hummed as she adjusted in the seat. "You probably want something fancy."

"No," Roman countered. "I prefer something good," he smiled as he leaned over and pressed his shoulder against hers.

"Well, if that's the case, I've got the perfect place in mind."

L'Arbre, her sister's restaurant, was the destination. The car ride was tinged with reserved excitement and a little bit of sexual tension. Yet, conversation flowed easily between

Roman and Ivory. Their proximity, however, didn't cause the excited tension to dissipate. The casual touch here, the accidental contact there only heightened the tenseness. And when they fell silent, with stolen glances being exchanged, the electricity between the two was palatable.

"What," Ivory flushed when she caught Roman staring at her.

"I just can't believe it," Roman replied, not caring that she caught him. "After all this time, and you still look as amazing as ever."

"Thank you," Ivory sighed.

But he didn't stop staring. Roman's gaze was penetrating as he searched Ivory's eyes, seemingly peering into her soul.

"What?" She asked again as she melted under his gaze. She looked away; her mink lashes fluttering against her caramel skin.

"I would apologize for staring," Roman began, "but that would be disingenuous. I'm just," he started but didn't continue. Roman didn't want to come on too strong and possibly scare Ivory off. He took a deep breath and then turned towards the window, reeling himself back in from saying too much too soon. He never told Ivory how he felt about her before. She put him in the friend zone, and he stayed there throughout high school. Roman accepted his place in her life. He would rather have Ivory in some capacity than not have her in his world at all. But that didn't stop him from loving her from afar, if you will. Seeing her again, reignited those old feelings full force, but not in a childish way. The resurgence was full grown. But it was too soon to be expelling her virtues and pouring out his heart.

Roman had to take a step back and just relax and try to enjoy the moment, not idolizing the past but focusing on the present.

Slowly, Roman turned back towards Ivory. He could tell she was nervous and possibly struggling with the same quandaries he was. No matter, though. He was determined to make the most of the time they had together, learning everything about her and enjoying her company.

When the car pulled up to the restaurant, Ivory had second thoughts. Not about spending time with Roman. Truthfully, she was curious about him, the man that sat next to her. Ivory got nervous because she wondered how many of her relatives could be inside the L'Arbre. It would be a complete disaster if they were to run into any of her sisters or cousins for that matter. They would stare, and point and comment, and maybe even come over to the table, asking the most embarrassing and inappropriate questions possible.

"Everything okay," Roman asked as he watched Ivory's eyes dart back and forth.

"Uh, yeah," Ivory muttered, offering Roman a wayward smile. Before she could voice her objection to going in, the driver was already at the door, opening it for her and Roman. He exited the limousine first and then extended a firm hand to help her out.

"Thank you," Ivory hummed as she stepped out onto the sidewalk.

"New place?" Roman asked as they walked towards the entrance.

"My sister's place," Ivory admitted.

"Really," Roman asked, making sure he walked on the

outside of Ivory between her and the street. "It has to be Kennedy's."

Ivory pivoted on her heels as her pace paused.

"What makes you say that?" She asked with a pitched brow.

"Come on, Ivory," Roman guffawed. "She's been cooking and baking since we were kids!"

Ivory thought about it for a moment, and he was right. For as long as she could remember, Kennedy was in the kitchen, under their mother's feet, asking bunches of questions and trying her hand at everything food related. When the rest of the girls were outside playing or hanging out with their friends, Kennedy was in the kitchen.

"Why do you think I was always trying to come over after school and stuff," Roman asked.

"Oh, I thought it was to hang out with me," Ivory quipped.

"It was," Roman smiled, "but that wasn't the only reason."

"Really now?"

"For real," Roman smiled. "I never left the Moore house hungry. Between your mom and your sister, my belly was always full. And, there were always homemade cookies in the cookie jar."

"Oh, my God!" Ivory squealed. "That was the ugliest clown cookie jar in the world!"

"That might be true," Roman agreed. "But it had the best cookies in it."

Ivory popped her lips and turned on her heels.

"And all this time, I thought it was me."

"And good food," Roman teased.

"Uhm," she huffed, pushing against Roman's arm. His response was exaggerated, and he stumbled over, even though she really didn't move him.

Ivory couldn't help but laugh.

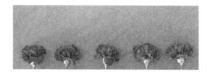

# Chapter Six

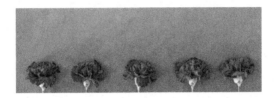

"**Y**ou make me sick," she huffed. "Just like old times."

"Damn straight," Roman laughed.

They were still laughing by the time they reached the door to L'Arbre. All worries about who might be inside were no longer on Ivory's mind. She was too busy having a good time with her old friend. Of course, when she entered the establishment, the hostess recognized her immediately and led the couple to a choice table. As they made their way through, Ivory did scope out the place to see if there were certain familiar faces. She almost didn't notice Roman pulling out the chair for her. Even as she sat down, Ivory still looked around. It was only when Roman sat next to her, and she felt his presence did Ivory return her attention to him. Not seeing family did help Ivory to relax.

"I'll take your drink orders when you're ready," the waitress said as she offered the duo menus to look over.

"Is it too early for champagne," Roman asked Ivory as the waitress walked away.

"I don't know," she replied. "Is there such a thing?"

"Ha," Roman laughed. "A woman after my own heart."

Roman picked up the menu and looked over the offerings. Ivory didn't need to. She already knew what she wanted. Anything either of them selected, Ivory was confident would be good. She'd eaten enough of it.

"What do you recommend," Roman asked. "Everything looks amazing."

Ivory leaned in and looked at his menu. The closer she got to him, the faster her heart pounded. "There are no bad choices," she commented. "It all depends on what you're in the mood for."

"What I'm in the mood for," Roman crooned. His gaze shifted from the printed words on the page to the beautiful woman sitting close enough to him to touch. Roman gained her eyes and held her gaze with his own. He folded his full lips in and released them slowly, all the while inhaling Ivory through his eyes.

"Stop it," Ivory hummed.

"What," he whispered.

"You know."

Roman's eyes narrowed and remained fixed on her.

There was intense heat that flushed Ivory's cheeks as her lids slowly batted. Once again, there was something about the way he said what he said that sent a chill down Ivory's spine. That, accompanied by the way Roman consumed her with his eyes, rendered Ivory weakened. It felt like her heart dropped to her belly; the sensation was so pervasive. Neither of them noticed when the waitress returned. She stood there for a moment without interrupting what was obviously a moment, so obvious, it made her smile. The waitress turned away, considering whether she should come back later. The amorous electrified energy between the couple made her feel like she was eavesdropping on a private moment.

"We apologize," Roman said, seeing the waitress in his periphery.

"No problem," the waitress smiled. Her cheeks were just about as warm as Ivory's. "Are you two ready to order, or should I come back?"

Ivory was grateful for the reprieve while simultaneously feeling embarrassed that the moment was witnessed by someone else.

"We're ready," Ivory smiled. What was worse is that she was familiar with the waitress who had been with the restaurant since the beginning. Roman had his head down, so he didn't see the wink the waitress gave Ivory or her mouthing, *He's hot,* which served to embarrass Ivory completely. Roman perused the menu one last time.

"I still can't decide," he murmured, looking to Ivory for assistance.

"Is there anything you're allergic to," she asked, daring to engage his eyes one more time.

"You don't remember?" Roman challenged with a sly grin.

Ivory's brow furrowed as she searched her memory.

"That was a long time ago," she whined as Roman searched her eyes challenging her.

A deep sigh passed through Ivory's full lips, and she

blinked slowly as she combed their history. She felt the waitress watching her too.

"Ah!" She exclaimed, offering a knowing smile of her own. "Peanuts!" She declared triumphantly.

"Mmhmm," Roman chortled.

"How could I forget that!" Now, Ivory was the one wearing a sly grin, and to his detriment, Roman knew why. It was certainly an inside joke that need not be discussed in front of the waitress. But Ivory had every intention of revisiting the matter.

"Surprise us," Ivory said to the waitress.

"We can do that," she answered. "And no peanuts!"

Ivory could barely contain the giggle that pranced on her lips as the waitress walked away.

"So, you remember, huh," Roman asked, knowing he was walking into it full on.

"I do," Ivory laughed. "It took me a minute, but, oh boy, do I remember," Ivory guffawed.

She turned to Roman again. This time, he was the one flushed with embarrassment, and Ivory loved every minute of it.

"What was her name again?"

"Seriously?" Roman asked. "Oh, so now you want to take that trek back down memory lane."

"Damn straight, Ivory quipped. She couldn't stop giggling. "What was her name again? Hmm," Ivory continued. "Don't tell me!"

"Trust me, I won't," Roman answered, remembering all too well the person Ivory was thinking about.

She placed her finger to her delicate chin and lifted her

eyes upwards, searching her mind for the name to that familiar face.

"Was it Bertha?" Ivory teased.

"Really," Roman laughed.

"She did have that big ole butt," Ivory chimed.

"She did," Roman admitted. Ivory's laughter was contagious, and although she did so at his expense, Roman couldn't help but join in.

"Cherry," Ivory exclaimed, clapping her hands together. "That was her name, Cherry Simpson! Who could forget her," Ivory sassed? "I know you can't, sir."

"Probably not," Roman answered. "And you're not going to let me, are you?"

"Uh nope," Ivory squealed. "You were crazy about Cherry in high school, remember that?"

Roman nodded and shook his head from the truth of that statement.

"You just had to have her, didn't you? She was all you talked about. Eye-balling her every chance you got, making sure you were near her locker when we changed classes. Then, you finally got that kiss," Ivory continued, "the one you'd been waiting for, not knowing she had had a peanut butter and jelly sandwich for lunch. Your lips swole up so big behind that. And then you started choking and gagging in the middle of the hallway like she had the cooties!?! Oh, my God! That thing was hilarious!"

"Mmhmm," Roman hummed. "The fact that I almost died didn't matter, though, did it?"

Ivory covered her mouth with both hands, trying to quell the giggle bubbling up in her soul.

"I cared," she smiled. "But once it was clear that you were fine..."

"Yeah, you and everybody else laughed your asses off," Roman huffed. He wrapped his arm around Ivory's waist and pulled her into him, teasing her for laughing at him, then and now. That contact, that innocuous touch, although all in good fun, sent a surge of powerful energy coursing between the two of them. It was like fire meeting fire head on; igniting and enkindling the more they remained connected.

"We did," Ivory chuckled. "We did."

Roman's touch. It countered the laugh on her lips with a spark in her soul. Ivory had never felt that kind of energy, that kind of spontaneous urgency with anyone else. It felt so good, not just to her body. It was more than that. It felt good to Ivory's soul. Yet, she refused to be presumptuous and read more into the feeling than may truly be there. Maybe it was merely nostalgia, a reconnection with the familiar that made it feel so right? Maybe she had been so long without the touch of a man that any tough would send her over the edge? Maybe... Roman's heart pumped hard. Ivory felt so good in his arms. Her smile was even more beautiful than he remembered, and the sound of her laughing, unreserved, natural and real, was music to his ears. Roman dealt with so many people who were fake; agreeing with him, kowtowing to him because of who he was, and the money he represented. They were far from real, far from genuine. Being with Ivory was refreshing, and Roman was enjoying every minute of it.

The waitress came just in time, with backup. The movement around him drew Roman's attention.

"Wow," Roman sighed as the waitress set several offerings on the table.

"For your enjoyment, we have the chef's choice," she announced. "Enjoy."

Their eyes feasted on the array of shi-shi-soul cuisine set before them, including a fresh salad to cleanse the palate prawns and grits, chicken and shrimp etouffee, chargrilled oysters on the half shell, and homemade French bread great for dipping.

"This looks amazing," Roman replied as he inhaled the amazing scents.

"I told you, L'Arbre doesn't disappoint," Ivory replied.

Roman placed the linen napkin across his lap and waited until Ivory had done the same. "Before we eat, would you allow me to say grace," he asked.

"Of course," Ivory agreed, impressed that he thought enough to do so.

Roman placed an upturned hand on the table and waited to receive Ivory's. He gently folded his fingers around hers as they both bowed their heads for prayer.

"Creator, we thank you for bringing us together for such a time as this. Thank you for the food and the hands that have prepared it. May it be nourishment to our bodies and our time together, nourishment to our souls. Amen."

"Amen," Ivory whispered.

"Now, let's eat," Roman encouraged. He still held on to Ivory's hand unconsciously. She didn't immediately pull away from him. After all, they had been friends for years. This was not like being with a stranger on a first date. This was familiar. Roman was like family to Ivory and the same for her. She knew him well. Conversation over dinner was just as light and lively as it had been the entire evening. The two revisited past times and enjoyed reconnecting.

"So, I have to ask," Ivory said, dabbing the corners of her mouth. "What are you up to now? Clearly, you've done well for yourself."

Roman held up a cautionary finger as he took another big bite of the etouffee. Ivory smiled and giggled a little. His face said it all.

"This is so good," Roman mumbled behind his hand. "Man."

Roman leaned back in his seat as he continued to chew, with his face reflecting just how much he enjoyed what he was eating. Ivory watched him happily, and then reached over with her napkin, finding a clean spot, and dabbing the corner of Roman's lips, where there was a little something left.

"Thank you," Roman smiled as he slid his arm on the back of Ivory's chair as he leaned forward. Ivory tending to him was sweet, and he didn't take it for granted. "What was your question again?"

"What have you been up to?" Ivory repeated. She started to get the feeling that maybe Roman didn't want to answer the question. Yet, she was willing to wait and see.

"Working, traveling," Roman replied.

"Okay," Ivory replied, "but that tells me absolutely nothing."

"I would much rather talk about what's going on with you," he iterated.

"Work and more work," Ivory answered.

"No, someone special?" Roman probed.

"I could ask you the same thing," Ivory quipped.

"That tells me nothing," Roman mimicked.

"Touché," Ivory grinned.

Wait staff returned. "Can we clear these?"

"Absolutely," Ivory replied. The interruption was a nice reprieve from the cat and mouse game the two were playing. Once the table was cleared, their original waitress returned.

"Compliments of the chef," she announced, placing homemade beignets with caramel drizzle and fresh strawberries in front of the duo.

The couple thanked them before the wait staff exited.

"I'm so full right now," Ivory sighed, rubbing her belly. "But, these are to die for."

"We must," Roman encouraged, picking up a warm beignet and offering the first bite to Ivory.

"Nnhnn," she whimpered as he moved the sweet treat closer to her luscious lips.

"Come on," he crooned with hooded eyes.

Roman gave her little choice as his deep baritone voice urged her on. Opening her mouth, she allowed Roman to feed her, and he watched as her lips brushed smoothly around the delicacy. Ivory's lashes fluttered against her bronze skin as she eased back. This time, it was Roman who attended to her, gently wiping a bit of powdery sugar from her bottom lip. Immediately, Ivory went to cover her mouth, but Roman was already there, shielding her attempt.

"Let me," he chortled. It wasn't a question. Ivory acquiesced.

Once again, there was a moment between the two

where everyone else around them faded to the background, and it was just them – Roman and Ivory in a space and time they created. She was mesmerizing, and although Roman cautioned himself earlier not to get caught up in who he knew her to be, it was hard. The woman that sat before him was more than the young girl he was infatuated with. Ivory struggled in much the same way. She had always been fond of Roman, amorously. But what she felt in the moment was more than fondness, friend- zoneness, if that was even a word. There was such an intensity of emotions and merging auras that it made it hard for Ivory to breathe. Bearing the penetration of Roman's gaze proved more difficult than that. But he didn't stop, drinking her in through his eyes, seizing her soul with his penetrating gaze.

*Stop it*, she mouthed, attempting to dissuade his consumption. Roman was having none of it and shook his head, making sure she knew just that. There was a part of him that couldn't help it; that still couldn't believe Ivory, his Ivory, was sitting right there with him after all this time.

"Are you ready to get out of here," Roman proposed.

"Sure," Ivory answered.

Roman signaled for the waitress to pay the check. She responded promptly, bringing it right over. Ivory was relieved for two reasons: the waitress's presence drew Roman's attention away from her, and it looked like they would get out of the restaurant without running into any family members. When the waitress approached, Roman didn't even look at the bill. Instead, he placed his black card in the folded bill case and handed it back to the waitress.

"I hope that just because we're finished eating, it doesn't mean you're finished with me," Roman suggested.

"What did you have in mind," Ivory asked as she mindlessly played with one of her curly tresses.

"I don't care what we do," Roman replied. "I just want to spend some more time with you... catching up, you know?"

Ivory lifted and lowered her shoulders and smiled. She heard what Roman said and what he intended. Truthfully, she felt the same way. Ivory couldn't remember the last time she'd had fun like this, with a guy. It wasn't awkward like a typical first date. There weren't all the mindless questions that led to nowhere, while all the while, the guy was marking time to make his first move that she would inevitably reject. And then there would be other awkward moments ending up with the date ending with a promise to keep in touch when neither of them really had the intention to. A cosmic waste of time that Ivory would just as soon avoid. Being with Roman didn't feel like that at all. And it didn't matter what they did next. Ivory was down for it.

"I guess I can hang out with you for a little longer," Ivory teased.

When the waitress returned, she had more than just Roman's credit card.

"I thought I would package this up for you two to take with you."

"That was so thoughtful," Ivory commented as she accepted the carryout bag. "Thank you."

"Thank you," Roman echoed as he reached in his back pocket and pulled out cash for her tip. He folded it and placed the cash in the waitress's hand.

"Oh my," she said, surprised by the amount. "Thanks so much!"

The waitress left, smiling. Ivory recognized Roman's generosity of spirit. Not from what she had witnessed presently, but from what she knew of him historically. He had always been giving, even when he was down to his last. That was part of what endeared her to him in their youth. She was happy to see that even though Roman physically changed, that part of his character hadn't.

## Chapter Seven

*R*oman lifted himself from the chair, standing to his full height. Immediately, he reached down and eased Ivory's chair back so she could stand as well. Roman picked up the bag the waitress left, and the duo proceeded towards the exit. Ivory flushed as she felt the strength of his hand again to the small of her back. That firm, supportive touch connected them. She felt like it was Roman's way of protecting her, keeping her close, although he was beside her. As they reached the door, it opened before Roman had an opportunity to reach for the handle. Politely, Ivory and Roman stepped to the side to allow those coming in to enter.

"Excuse u-."

Trinity's words stopped short in her throat as she was surprised by her sister. Tempestt, who was following close behind, paused as well. Before they could say more, both Trinity's and Tempestt's eyes traveled from Ivory to the handsome man behind her then back to Ivory, whose mouth was agape, and eyes were wide. Trinity could just about read Ivory's mind. *Please don't make a scene, please don't make a scene.* Trinity contemplated her next move with a sinister smile. Ivory's eyes grew even wider. Roman stood back, unsure as to what was happening. He couldn't see Ivory's face, just the faces of the two women standing in front of him.

"Hey, sis," Trinity purred. Behind her, Tempestt offered a too cute little way that was pure snark.

"Hey," Ivory mumbled, attempting to take a step forward to avoid any further conversation.

"Sis," Roman asked, his velvety baritone voice musically tantalizing all three women's ears. The smiles on Trinity and Tempestt's faces grew even wider. They had to know who this mystery man was and had no intention of leaving until they did.

Ivory's eyes rolled in her head. She knew there was no other option but to make introductions. With an extended arm and killer smile, Roman encouraged the trio to move out of the doorway so further conversation could commence.

"Roman, this is my kid sister, Trinity, and our cousin Tempestt."

Before Roman could greet the ladies, Trinity threw up a cautionary hand.

"Roman?" She asked, looking up at him again. She couldn't even balk at the kid sister response she was so taken aback by who he was. Ivory and Trinity were very close in age, so Trinity remembered Roman well. Because he was

Ivory's friend, he was like Trinity's friend, too. "Lil' Rommie Rom from back in the day Roman?"

He had to laugh. It was the second time that evening Roman was reminded of who he was in the past and just how vertically challenged he had been.

"Yes, Trinity, it's me, Romy Rom," he countered with a chuckle.

Ivory died a little inside. She didn't want the two of them to start trekking down memory lane, especially when she was so close to coming out of the evening unscathed by a familial encounter. Trinity didn't know what Ivory was thinking, nor did she really care. She had fond memories of Roman being at the family home, sneaking her fresh baked cookies when he snuck some for himself. Ivory's natural predilection was to smile widely and open her arms to him for a big ole hug. Roman was glad for the kind extension of familiarity and graciously hugged her in return.

"Nice to meet you as well," Roman offered, extending a gentlemanly hand to Tempestt, who he was not as familiar with. Ivory prayed the conversation would die there, and she practically inserted herself into their shared commentary to make sure that is precisely what happened.

"See ya'll later," Ivory said as she reached for Roman's hand to usher him out. She couldn't allow her face to show her body's reaction to his enclosed touch to her flesh. That would be food for fodder and Ivory refused to add any fuel to what could become a burning flame for Trinity and Tempestt to torment her about later. But Roman felt it and squeezed Ivory's hand just a little bit tighter to make sure she knew he was there.

"Mmhmm," Trinity quipped with a wink. "We will definitely see you later."

The look on Tempestt's face echoed the same sarcastic, sassy sentiment. Ivory would have a lot to answer to the next time she ran into those two again. By the time she and Roman made it to the street, Ivory was damn near dragging Roman. He didn't mind, but it was kind of funny.

"Can we slow down now," Roman chortled, curtailing his pace which inevitably slowed hers.

"Yeah," Ivory snickered, considering what she must have looked like to any bystander.

"What was that all about," Roman asked, although he probably knew the answer.

"Nothin'," Ivory whined. She pouted, with her lips stuck out. It was cute, but that's not what Roman was thinking. With one smooth move, he reeled Ivory back into him, still maintaining the warming hold he had on her hand.

"Are you embarrassed to be seen with me?"

"No," Ivory sighed, melding into the strength of his core, her hand naturally falling against the rise of his sculpted chest.

Roman waited until her eyes traveled to where he could connect with them. And once again, time stood perfectly still as Roman gazed into Ivory's dark brown eyes, and she looked up into his. All movement on the street ceased as the dim glow from the streetlight highlighted Ivory's incredible silhouette.

"Are you sure?" Roman inquired with a gentle finger under Ivory's chin, inclining her to him even more.

That touch... it was sensory overload, and Ivory

squirmed under the scathing pressure. This she couldn't have imagined, not with her old friend.

"I'm sure," she whispered, pressing her thighs closely together to try and quiet the pulse she felt in her jewel. There was a part of Ivory that wanted to pull away; to move away from Roman because of how he made her feel so unexpectedly, so wanton. Yet, there was another part of Ivory that wanted to stay just where she was, close to him in a new and intriguing way. The conflict was palatable. She'd never been a girl that just went with the moment, impromptu, adventurous, especially with matters of the heart. Ivory was a thinker and sometimes an overthinker, maybe to her detriment. Just riding with whatever was not what she was used to. Just maybe, it was time for a change... at least a little one.

"So, what do you want to do now," Ivory asked. She needed to get out of her own head.

"It's nice out," Roman replied. "Will you walk with me?"

"Sure," Ivory smiled.

Roman extended his hand, and within an instant, the driver was there, retrieving the bags from the restaurant. Roman didn't have to explain himself, and the driver didn't ask. He was there at Mr. West's beckon call. Roman kept Ivory close, still holding one hand as he wrapped his arm around her waist. She didn't balk or push away, instead, falling in perfect sync with him. Her stride was decidedly shorter than his and Roman made the adjustment to accommodate her. The evening was nice. There was a gentle breeze, and the sun had just kissed the horizon. There was a slight spattering of orange color giving way to midnight blue as night took over day. They didn't talk for a while, strolling side by side, feeling each other's movement, recognizing their synchronized progression. All the tired that Ivory felt earlier in the day was gone. She felt an energy that surpassed any prior feeling.

Roman appreciated that the silence between them was not in the least bit awkward. Instead, it was peaceful, not tinged with any kind of anxiety or pressure to fill the blankness of the space. That kind of calm only came with the right person. In so many ways, Roman had always known Ivory was just right. As they neared a bench, Roman invited Ivory to sit. She acquiesced, and he made sure she was comfortable before taking his place beside her. They were close, just enough to remain physically connected to each other, which Roman liked. He wanted that; to remain connected to Ivory. He'd missed her in the ten years or so that they'd been apart, thinking of her often over the years, and always fondly. He didn't want to experience that missing feeling again.

"I have a confession to make," Roman started.

Ivory's furrowed brow showed how intrigued she was. "Really?"

"Mmhmm," Roman hummed.

A thousand thoughts ran through Ivory's mind, and many of them weren't good. Maybe he was going to tell her that he was married, or engaged, or had a long-term lover he was thinking of marrying. Maybe he had a dark past that he figured it was important to share. Maybe... There were a million maybes. Ivory searched Roman's eyes to see if they were truly windows to his soul. She wanted to see whether his soul was darker than she ever knew or whether there were secrets there she might not want to hear. She felt a pit in her stomach growing. The anxiety she felt in the moment was surreal and so out of order. Roman owed her nothing. They were old friends, accidently reacquainted. Why was Ivory's stomach churning and the tiny hairs on the back of her neck standing on end? Roman's eyes gave very little away. His gaze was as deep and penetrating as it had ever been stealing her breath away the longer it lasted. This time, though, Ivory didn't disengage. She continued to search for answers in the split second before Roman started to speak.

"You asked me earlier what I had been up to," Roman began, still giving very little away.

Ivory's heart was beating erratically in her chest, so much so that she quietly blew out a long breath between pursed lips.

"Yeah, I did," she answered.

"Well," Roman began and then paused, far too long for Ivory's liking.

"Well, what?"

She knew it was going to be bad news. Ivory could feel it in her gut. Maybe she shouldn't have asked. Maybe he shouldn't have waited so damn long to answer the question. He wouldn't wait if it was good, right?

"I am working in the family business."

Ivory's brow wrinkled again. "What?"

She'd never known Roman's family to have a business. Maybe this was new.

"Okay," she muttered. "And what business is that?"

"Well, to be honest," Roman began. Ivory didn't like another hesitation in his speech. Starting with 'I have a confession to make' and all these damn long ass pauses was irking her soul. *Just get it over with already*, she thought. *Who is she*, is what Ivory was really thinking.

"We've been in business a long time," Roman continued. "Even when we were in school together."

"Okay," Ivory replied curiously.

"It's a billion-dollar business," Roman went on.

"Wait, hold on," Ivory mumbled. Roman was so sketchy with the information Ivory had to figure out what he was trying to tell her, and why it was taking him so long to do it.

"Has your family's business always been a billion-dollar business? What kind of business?"

"Yes," Roman replied. "International finance."

"Even when we were in school," Ivory repeated.

"Yes," he answered again.

Ivory's arm lifted, and she rested her elbow on her leg, balancing her chin on her hand as she put two and two together. Roman could literally see the wheels turning in her head. He wasn't sure how she would react to him or think of him when she finally connected the dots.

"The public school that we attended," she mused.

"Yes, Ivory," Roman confessed.

She fell quiet again, and Roman didn't have a good feeling. This could undermine everything they had in the past, and everything that could potentially happen from here on out. Ivory lifted her head and looked at him again. Roman couldn't tell whether it was disapprovingly or inquisitively. The darkness of the evening didn't help any either. It was so hard to read Ivory's face.

# CELESTE GRANGER

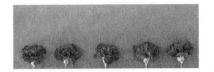

# Chapter Eight

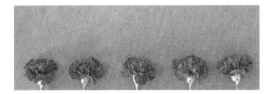

"You've always been rich, huh? Is that what you're trying to tell me? That you've always been from a wealthy family?" Ivory didn't know whether to laugh or frown. His surprise was rather disarming, and it made her think about their time together in school, how much time they spent together, when and where they spent time together. How could she not have known?

Was that judgment in her voice? Disapproval?

"Let me explain," Roman iterated.

"Don't explain yet," Ivory interrupted. "Just answer the question, Roman. It's simple, yes or no?"

It was Roman who sighed this time. She didn't give him much choice or much opportunity to respond the way he wanted to.

"Yes," he said flatly. He wanted to be hopeful that Ivory would respond favorably, but Roman wasn't sure. Money could change everything; it could change people and how people are viewed. He didn't want Ivory to see him differently. He was cool with her knowing that as an adult, he was wealthy; yet, that knowledge now of his history could be bad. His confession meant that he had been less than honest with Ivory the whole time she had known him. Their prior existence, to a certain degree, had been built on falsehoods. That could be catastrophic for their friendship. He had hidden so much of who he was the entire time. But he couldn't presuppose what was going on in her head. All Roman could do was wait and see what the fallout would be.

Slowly, Ivory lifted her head from her hand. she leaned away from him for the first time since they'd been together. Roman's shoulders dropped just a little, and his eyes fell away from hers. He folded his lips in and slightly shook his head. Nope, he didn't have a good feeling about this.

When Ivory punched him hard in the arm, Roman balked, turning back towards her with wide eyes.

"Ouch," he groaned, rubbing the place where she hit him.

"I should hit you again," Ivory scolded, tightening her eyes and staring him down.

He didn't ask her why. Instead, Roman waited, now searching her eyes for any inclination as to what she really thought about what he said.

"Can I explain," he dared to ask.

"I don't need an explanation from you, sir," Ivory quipped.

"Please..."

"Uh, nope," she snapped, still giving nothing away with her eyes.

Ivory turned away, straightforward, and folded her arms underneath her ample chest. This time when she fell silent, and there was nothing but silence between them, it was uncomfortable, tinged with tense emotionality. That silence seemed to go on forever with no relief in sight. He didn't press, though. He had to give Ivory space to process what he said in whatever way she needed to. It was a lot, and it was impactful. Roman knew he had to allow Ivory to absorb it and whatever his confession meant to her.

"You mean to tell me that instead of taking the bus, we could have been riding in a stretch limo?"

Her inquiry was rhetorical, requiring no response from him.

When she giggled, Roman instantly felt a tiny bit of relief. When she punched him again, he was able to chuckle with her.

"Nnhnn," she groaned. "Why didn't you tell me?"

Because," Roman began. He was chuckling, but his laugh slowly faded. Ivory unfolded her arms and turned in his direction.

"Because what, Roman?"

He had a distant look in his eyes, and Ivory began to get a glimpse of why he had held on to his secret for so long.

"It sounds silly now, but I just wanted to fit in." His tone was revealing and somber. There was a sensitivity there that Ivory hadn't seen from Roman before, not when it came to himself.

"That makes sense," Ivory began. "But with me, Roman? What, did you think I would look at you differently?"

"Honestly? Yes," he answered. "Not because you were

shallow or anything like that," Roman explained. "I never thought that. And at one point, I thought about telling you. But I didn't want it to change anything, how you looked at me, how you saw me, how you knew me."

There was a snippy reply on Ivory's lips, but she withheld it, hearing the sincerity and honesty in his voice. She had to accept how he felt about the situation at the time. Of course, present tense, it was easy to say that his wealth and means wouldn't have made a difference. Truthfully, though, maybe it would have; maybe she would have seen him differently, treated him differently. Those things they had in common, the things their friendship had been built on may have looked different had she known he was affluent. She reserved her comment. She'd grown from the girl she had been. She couldn't look back through womanly eyes.

"I feel you," Ivory finally answered. "I do," she continued.

"Does that change things, though," Roman asked cautiously and then almost immediately regretted even raising the question. Because if the answer was yes, everything he thought, everything he hoped for their rekindling might be all for naught.

"It does," Ivory acknowledged.

Roman's heart sank, slowly and deeply in his chest. The worst of what he thought might be what was coming to pass.

She felt a shift in his energy and saw that his head had dropped slightly. She didn't want that and quickly moved to correct the situation, placing a gentle finger to his strong chin and lifting it slightly until he was able to look at her again.

"Not in the way you think," Ivory reassured.

He dared to be hopeful as she continued.

"I do feel some type of way because you didn't tell me, Ivory began. Yet, I can't look at the situation from here. I have to accept that you had your reasons for doing what you did. I just wish I could have been the kind of friend you felt like you could share something that big with, knowing it wouldn't have changed anything." Ivory paused and then continued. "I can respect that you didn't know that for sure."

"And I didn't want to lose you," Roman replied. "I didn't want to lose what we had. It was so pure, and..."

His voice fell away with the discontinuation of what he wanted to say.

"Go on," she encouraged, not sure if she was ready for what he hesitated to say. He paused because he always paused when it came to being honest with Ivory, revealing his truest self to her. This time was no different. Roman had already risked undermining their relationship, he wasn't sure whether he should do it again with another revelation, despite how honest it was. Ivory could read hesitation all over him.

"Don't hold back now, she encouraged.

"Are you sure about that," Roman questioned; the sexy in his voice returning full on.

"Now, I'm not sure," Ivory confessed, feeling the wave of his baritone wash all over her. Nervously, she uncrossed and crossed her shapely legs again, waiting to hear what Roman had to say.

"I loved you," he admitted. "I was in love with you."

The furrow that once inhabited Ivory's brow gave way to surprise.

"What? Nah," she declared, waving a playfully dismissive hand in Roman's direction.

But he was not to be dismissed. Reaching for her hand, Roman secured it in his own and gained her full attention with his touch and his words.

"Seriously, Ivory," he confessed. "I was in love with you the entire time."

"But you never said anything," she smiled giddily because she didn't know what else to do. "It feels like you never said a lot of things." Her intonation was more somber and reserved as the thought of the secrets played out in her mind.

"I didn't share my feelings for you for the same reason as I didn't share my family's history," Roman explained. "I didn't want to lose you, no matter what. You meant just that much to me."

"It was puppy dog love, right? That infatuation kind," she reasoned aloud with a lift of her shoulders and a wide smile. She could accept that. All kids had those kinds of feelings about one person or another.

"No, not at all," Roman replied without hesitation. "It was the biggest, realest feeling I ever had in my life." She observed Roman again. There was no chuckle behind it or toying in his voice. He was dead ass serious, and everything about him said so.

"Wow," was all Ivory could say as she replayed so many shared moments in her head.

"You're serious, right?" She asked trepidatiously.

"Very," he answered.

Wow, she thought in her head but didn't repeat out loud.

Roman drew small circles with his thumb to the back of Ivory's hand. They were both lost in their own thoughts, contemplating the thoughts of the other. So much had been unpacked in such a short period of time, Ivory wasn't sure what to do with most of it. But to think that Roman was in love with her, like for real in love was somewhat flattering, yet unreal and a little unsettling because he never ever said anything. And then she thought about it some more. Although Roman was decidedly shorter than she was, especially in junior high, he never let that stop him from trying to protect her, look out for her, be the big brother she never knew she needed or wanted – not in a sibling kind of way in as much as in an I'm here for you no matter what kind of way. Roman had always made Ivory his priority, she thought, because they were the best of friends. He sacrificed for her, accommodated her, did things he probably didn't want to do like watch romantic comedies and eat popcorn on a Saturday afternoon because that's what she wanted to do. Roman never ceased to make Ivory feel important to him. She figured he was just a really good friend and an overall good dude. She never thought there was more to it than that because there didn't need to be more. He was enough, her best friend, period.

But to hear Roman tell it, love was the undercurrent that made all of the above possible. He loved her, not like a sister, but romantically loved her. More than that, he was willing to sacrifice and subdue his true feelings for her because he loved her so much. That was a big emotion, a huge grown folk type of action or inaction to take, and it was all because of how he cared for her.

Instead of being unsettled by his newest admission, Ivory was instead overwhelmed by it. And the more she thought about what Roman being in love with her truly meant, the more Ivory's heart beat for him. It was uncanny.

"Say something, Ivory, please."

Roman didn't want to let her hand go. He didn't want to disconnect from her, not now.

"I don't know what to say," Ivory stammered. "I'm just floored."

She looked at Roman again. "Was I really that clueless?" She asked ashamedly.

"No," he affirmed. "It's not that you were clueless," Roman continued. "You just didn't consider it."

"I didn't have to," Ivory added. Then she thought about how that sounded and felt the need to expound on it. "You were always good to me, always," she added. "Any you were good for me," she continued, more as a personal revelation than an admission to him. "Huh, when you think about it, that's what love looks like," she mused.

When she looked into Roman's eyes, they sparkled in a way she hadn't seen. He slowly revealed a brilliantly, sexy smile that lit up his entire face. The fact that she understood was such a relief to Roman, he couldn't help but smile. This conversation could have gone sideways more than once, but it didn't, and for that, he was grateful. She got it. Ivory understood. And her understanding was reflected in every part of him as he rested his arm around the back of the bench, slightly cradling her shoulder. He wanted to hug her, hold her, pull Ivory in close and feel her flesh against his flesh, a reassurance that they were still good. But he didn't. the situation was still too tenuous for that.

"What," Roman asked, seeing Ivory shake her head while wearing a sheepish grin.

"I'm just," she began.

"Disappointed?"

"No, I wouldn't say that," Ivory rebuffed.

"Insulted?"

"No, not that either," she frowned.

"Relieved," Roman teased, pulling her into him and squeezing her shoulder lightly.

"Uh no," Ivory guffawed.

"Then what?" Roman pressed.

"Stunned, I think," Ivory mused. "I mean, you kept so much from me, important stuff. And I get why, for real, like there's no judgment in what I'm saying, but it does make me wonder how I could have missed so much."

Ivory paused contemplatively before continuing her train of thought.

"In some ways, I feel like I didn't really know you at all, but I did know you, you know. Do you see my quandary," she asked? "Like I knew you, but only the you I was allowed to see."

"Yeah, I get that," Roman answered. "Which is probably why I stayed silent for so long."

"Why are you telling me now, though?" Ivory questioned. "I mean, we could have gone on, with the memories we had, forever, with everything remaining just how we knew it."

"That's the thing, though," Roman replied. "It was just as

you knew it. So much of what I felt and who I was didn't enter into it."

That was a powerful statement that gave Ivory pause. Still, Roman craftily avoided answering her question. But what had her inquiries gained thus far? A bunch of new information Ivory still hadn't fully synthesized. It might be best if he didn't answer. There was still room for the answer to this question to be a bombshell one she might not be ready for. Yet, she wanted to know. Whether the answer was good, bad, or indifferent, Ivory had to know why he was spilling his guts now.

"You're telling me all of this because?"

"I thought you should know, the truth, my truth, the real truth."

"I can appreciate that," Ivory sighed. Maybe that was all, and if it was, Ivory was okay with it.

"Seeing you again, so unexpectedly, though, reminded me of so much," Roman said. "It reawakened so much of who I am, and what you have always meant to me."

Roman didn't say any more, instead, expressing his truest sentiment, by planting a loving kiss to the center of Ivory's forehead. The feel of his lips to her flesh in such an affectionate way sent a wave of warmth coursing through Ivory's body to the core of her soul. His kiss was intentional, and she felt his intention fully.

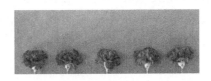

# Chapter Nine

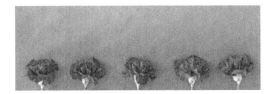

They talked for hours and could have talked for hours more. Time flew by so quickly as the conversation ebbed and flowed between the serious and the silly, the sublime and the ridiculously funny. After a while, Roman and Ivory started to walk again, at a leisurely pace, both thoroughly enjoying the company of the other. It truly felt like old times, when the two could talk about absolutely nothing in particular and just enjoy being together. Some of the tension from the earlier conversation seemed to wain the more they conversed. That was a relief to both of them, that they could continue to communicate like old friends. That was important and made Roman feel better about his disclosures; that what he shared hadn't ruined everything.

"There's one subject we have yet to discuss," Ivory began, as they strolled side by side down the boulevard.

"And what subject is that, pray tell," Roman mused.

"Why you're single," Ivory replied. "I assume you're single," she teased, lifting his large hand and examining it for a ring.

Playfully, Roman pulled his hand away. "I could ask you the same thing, ma'am," Roman scoffed, mimicking Ivory's action by reaching over and checking her ring finger. Ivory giggled, slapping his hand away. Roman reached for her, and she skirted his grasp, quickly padding ahead as though she intended to run from him. But Roman was having none of that. Before Ivory could get three steps ahead, she was lifted off her feet. He'd grabbed her around the waist with both hands and then twirled her in a circle until she was laughing out loud. That sound of unfiltered happiness was music to Roman's ears.

"Oh my God," she squealed. "Put me down!"

"Or what," Roman challenged, spinning her again. He was laughing too which only served to aggravate the already aggravated Ivory

"Roman, please," she chuckled. "Im'ma be dizzy!"

He acquiesced, but not without one more whirl that sent Ivory screaming with laughter. Gently he lowered her to her feet and made sure she was firmly planted before letting go.

"Woo," Ivory exclaimed, her eyes growing wide as she felt herself teetering too far to one side. Roman was right there to catch her, holding her firmly tucked in his strong arm.

"I gotchu," he affirmed as he held her tight.

"You better," Ivory chastised, elbowing him in the side. "I told you I was getting dizzy," she fussed.

"And I told you, I gotchu," Roman insisted.

"Fine!"

"You just have to have the last word, don't you," Roman countered. "Some things never change."

"Ugh," Ivory hissed. "You make me so sick," she chuckled because what Roman said was true.

"See what I mean?"

She was tempted to say something else. But that would have proven Roman right, and Ivory was not about to do that. It was hard, though. She had a snappy comeback that she proceeded to choke down to prove that his comment was incorrect. The struggle to remain silent was real, and Roman saw Ivory struggling.

"Go on and say it," he encouraged with a teasing smile. "You know you want to."

The eye roll she leveled in Roman's direction was ferocious, but it only made Roman laugh more.

"Ugh," Ivory bellowed, and then realized that although it wasn't a word per say, it was still an utterance Roman quickly quantified as verbiage, with a shrug of the shoulders and an accusatory point of the finger.

Teasingly, Ivory raised her hand as though she was once again a student in a classroom and impatiently waited for Roman to call on her. Of course, Roman made her wait, stretching it out as long as he could.

"Yes, Ivory," he replied formally, straightening up his face as best he could.

"You might as well take me back to my car, then," she pouted.

"Because you're tired of me?"

"Well," Ivory sighed, elongating her response to give

Roman pause. But Roman watched her nonverbals more than what Ivory said. She was rocking on her sensible heels, shifting her weight from one foot to the other, almost like a little shimmy. Her eyes were bright, although her tone was snarky, and there was a hint of a titillating smile flirting in the corners of her lips. Everything about the way she moved suggested that her words were contradictory to what she really wanted.

"Come here, girl," Roman said, not asking permission but rather reaching for Ivory with both hands and easing her into him. With his masculine arms wrapped around her feminine waist, Ivory was planted. The lack of resistance was a good sign, and instead of frowning and protesting, the smile that teetered on erupting, spread beautifully across her plump lips. Roman leaned down, eradicating the distance between them, and placed his lips against Ivory's ear.

"You sick of me," he chortled. The warmth of his minty breath pressed against Ivory's flesh sending showers of hot flames to her essence. She inhaled against his chest, breathing in his virile scent as his silky voice soothed her soul. Ivory's breathing became labored, panting as she felt his body pressed against hers. She was completely enveloped, cocooned by Roman, and her body responded viscerally, faster than her mind could contradict. Her lips formed the words to respond to Roman's question, yet nothing but air passed through her lips as she felt the expansion of his chest against her cheek. There was nothing but strength behind the tailored shirt he wore. Being in Roman's arms was comforting and salacious at the same time and it made it difficult for Ivory to think straight.

"Did you hear me, Ivory," Roman whispered even closer to her ear, his lips teasingly grazing her flesh. She visibly squirmed as her knees buckled under the weight of his intensity. Roman felt her weakening in his arms, and his body responded in kind, his nature rising, his sensibilities heightening, his arms holding onto her even tighter. A gasp escaped Ivory's lips as her body quaked against his. She didn't intend to utter the sound, but she couldn't help it. Roman had her weak for him.

He moved, his lips passing closely against her ear, around to her cheek, and then to her lips. He didn't kiss her; instead, Roman stayed there, just a whisper away from making contact, and asked the question again.

"Are... you... sick... of... me?"

Oh, the melodic whisper of his words, the warmth of his hum against Ivory's wanton lips, was more than Ivory could stand.

"Roman," she utters, feeling her jewel thump unrelentingly. Her breath against his lips is enough to remove any inhibition, any reservation he had left. He couldn't hold out any longer. He was willing to take his chances.

There was no space left between them as Roman closed the distance, first lightly grazing Ivory's lips. He just wanted to feel them against his own. His eyes closed as he savored the moment, a moment he'd waited for as long as he could remember. Roman languished in the moment; no rushing to kiss Ivory fully, but just to be that close to her, to touch her purely and innocently and feel her essence give in to his. It was torture for Ivory. Roman being that close, tantalizing and taunting her obliging lips sent a scurry of explosive fluttering's cascading through her. She needed him to kiss her, so much so that Ivory was tempted to end the torture and press her full lips against his. The moment was antagonizing. Ivory could feel her pearl releasing wetness, enough so that she had to clench her thighs to quiet the pulsations. It wasn't working.

"Please," she beckoned, unable to resist her natural predilections. Ivory's entire being seemed to be filled with anticipation.

Roman had no resistance left either. He kissed her, and Ivory's lips gave way to his, welcoming Roman in. His kiss sang through her veins, sending spirals of ecstasy through her. His lips covered her mouth, devouring its softness with hungry ravishings. Roman had waited so long for this, and it was everything he could have ever imagined it would be. His lips recaptured hers, sending the pit of Ivory's stomach into a whirl. His reclaiming crushed any hesitation Ivory had left, and she kissed him with an intensity that belied any outward calm. Neither of them wanted their entanglement to end, and their kiss was unrelenting, both of them giving into passions they'd never explored. They had always been friends, the best of friends. Yet, this kiss suggested that there was something more.

When Roman finally released her, sealing their impassioned kiss with a much gentler, dragging kiss, he dared to ask her again.

"Are you sick of me," still just an inkling from Ivory's mouth.

She looked up into Roman's dark, brooding eyes that encapsulated her fully.

"No," she breathed. "Not anymore..."

Roman's gaze was as soft as a caress, that was echoed by the way he held her.

# Chapter Ten

"I don't want you to go," Roman confessed after the duo returned to the limo. Their time together had been amazing, and Roman wanted their time to continue. Ivory was comfortably tucked in Roman's arms as the idling driver awaited instruction from Mr. West. Ivory's day had been long, but she didn't really want to go either. But she knew she needed to. Ivory's resistance was at an all-time low. She still couldn't believe the kiss that lingered on her lips. She still couldn't believe the emerging and completely unexpected feelings she had for her old friend.

"I have to, though," Ivory half-heartedly protested.

"I know," Roman sighed.

"My car's still at the office," Ivory reminded.

"I can take you home," Roman suggested, "and then take you to work in the morning."

They had been out all evening. The sun would be cresting in the morning sky in just a few hours.

"I appreciate the offer," Ivory replied, lifting slightly from her comfortable space nestled in Roman's arms. "But, I can drive myself."

He didn't want Ivory to have to, but he agreed. He instructed the driver to return to the embassy. The couple rode quietly, as Ivory settled back into the space, she previously occupied. Roman tilted his head slightly, feeling the wave of her curly tresses grazing his chin. The limo arrived back at the embassy much faster than Roman would have liked. Truthfully, the driver could have driven ten miles an hour, and it would have been too fast for Roman. As the driver prepared to exit the vehicle to open the back-passenger doors, Roman stopped him, advising that he would take care of it himself. Dutifully, the driver lifted the one-way glass that offered privacy to those in the back and kept the car in park. Roman waited until Ivory lifted herself from him before he moved to open the car door.

Although Roman's long strides could have gotten him to Ivory's door much faster, he wasn't in any hurry. He had no choice but to accept that their time together was over. All he could do was hope that he would have a chance to spend more time with Ivory sooner rather than later. Arriving on her side of the vehicle, Roman opened the door and extended his hand to assist Ivory out of the car. Gracefully, she eased out, and then stood to her full height, stepping aside so Roman could close the door behind her. Ivory's car was just a few feet away. Roman made sure that the driver parked close by. He wouldn't dare have her walking to a parking space alone.

Roman continued to hold Ivory's hand as they walked

over to her vehicle. Her pace closed as they arrived at the driver's side door.

"I could have taken you home," Roman reiterated.

"I know," Ivory answered.

Roman's head dropped slightly. He wasn't used to being told no, even if it was polite. Ivory smiled. She'd seen that pouty face before. Bending down in front of him, Ivory waited until she gained his eyes. How she could reduce him to pouting was uncanny and unnerving. But Roman didn't care. He refused to hide his true feelings from Ivory anymore, no matter how it made him look. She knew he was as Alpha as an Alpha man could be. Roman was willing to be a little vulnerable in her presence... just a little because he knew Ivory would never hold that against him or throw it in his face. She wasn't that kind of girl and certainly not that kind of woman.

Roman looked down into Ivory's smiling face and maintained her gaze as her eyes lifted his.

They examined each other before either of them spoke another word.

"Just don't say goodbye," Roman uttered.

"I won't," Ivory sighed. "I know you don't like that."

Dropping her gaze, Ivory rumbled through her small crossbody bag for her keys. When she pulled them out, Roman reached for them, and she politely placed them in his hand. He unlocked the car door but didn't immediately open it; dragging out their last few moments of time together. He truly did not want to let Ivory go. He'd done that once before, and they were apart for years.

"When are you leaving," Ivory asked, seeing his resistance and feeling some of it herself.

"That's up to you," Roman answered.

"That is so not fair," Ivory rebuffed.

"It's true, though." "Can I see you after work," Roman asked flashing Ivory an award-winning smile.

"I'm not sure what time I'll be off," Ivory replied.

"Is that a yes?"

"Yes, Roman," she smiled. "Where's your phone?"

Gladly, Roman reached into his jacket pocket and pulled out his phone, handing it to Ivory.

"It's not locked," she asked, after touching the power button.

"No reason to, Roman replied.

"Hmm, she hummed, which reminded Ivory of a question that remained unanswered on both their parts. She moved to the contacts and placed her number there.

"Let me save it," Roman suggested, reaching for his device.

"Why?" Ivory asked, teasingly pulling it back.

Roman didn't say anything else. He just left his extended hand and waited. His eyes were compelling, and Ivory was curious. She relinquished and placed the phone in Roman's hand. With a few clicks, the number was saved.

"What did you save it under," she asked curiously.

"Something special."

She had to live with his answer because Roman offered nothing more.

"Call me when you get a chance, so I'll have your number," Ivory suggested, preparing to enter the vehicle.

Roman nodded his head, resolved that their time together was just about over.

"Thank you for a wonderful day," she smiled.

"Thank you."

He wanted to kiss her again, to devour her succulent lips and hold her close just one more time. But Roman refrained from following his instinct. He didn't want to pressure Ivory by moving too fast. He didn't want to scare her off. She'd just become familiar with his feelings for her, so Roman didn't want to press it.

"I'll see you later," Roman smiled as he opened her car door and helped usher her in. His smile grew wider as Ivory leaned over and placed a sweet kiss on his cheek. He could have easily turned, and their lips would have met. And he did, just one last time, close enough to give Ivory something to think about. She would, for a long time.

Roman stood up and checked one last time to make sure Ivory was clear of the door before shutting it. He waited until she turned on the ignition before retreating to his own vehicle. Ivory watched as Roman returned to his car. she breathed in deeply and let out a long, slow sigh.

"Who would have ever thunk it," she mused aloud.

The day had been full of unpredictable surprises, more than Ivory could have dreamed.

"Lil Romy Rom," she uttered with a bright smile. Putting the car in gear, Ivory eased from the parking space as Roman disappeared into his own vehicle. Ivory didn't need the entertainment of her radio for the ride home. Her mind was filled with thoughts, ideas, and memories, some long past, and some more recent. All her thoughts involved Roman, the one she knew, and the one she was getting to know. Fortunately, there were not a lot of cars on the road, which made for an easy trek to her residence. As Ivory turned onto her street, she noticed a set of headlights turning with her. She didn't think a whole lot of it at first, but when she turned again towards her cul de sac, the lights turned again with her.

Ivory's eyes flitted from the street in front of her to the rearview mirror. It was still too dark to discern exactly what kind of car was behind her. She was just a few blocks away from her house. For the briefest moment, Ivory considered going past her driveway just to see what the car behind her would do. Instead, Ivory decided to slow down at the base of her driveway to see if she could get a glimpse of the car or who was in it. Fortunately, there was a streetlight nearby that would offer her a chance to get a good look.

Just then, Ivory's phone rang. The connection to her car lit up, so she didn't have to take her eyes off the road in order to answer. She didn't recognize the number, but given the hour, Ivory decided to answer it anyway.

"Yes?"

"It's me, babe," Roman crooned. "I should have told you I was going to follow you home to make sure you arrived safely."

"That's sweet, but you creeped the shit out of me," she laughed, breathing a sigh of relief.

"I promise to make it up to you," Roman's velvety voice sounded just as sexy through the surround sound in her car.

"I'm going to hold you to that."

"Promise?" Roman teased.

"Promise," she smiled.

"I'll wait until you are inside, okay?"

"Thanks," Ivory agreed.

"You don't need to thank me," Roman corrected. "It's the least I can do."

The line remained open as Ivory navigated into the driveway and pulled into the garage. Turning off the car, Ivory picked up her cell phone, maintaining their connection. Roman watched as the garage door closed and waited until there were signs of life inside. He could hear Ivory moving on the other end of the line.

"I'm turning off the alarm system," she said as she made her way through the connecting door.

"I'm still here with you," Roman reassured.

"I know," she smiled.

Roman could hear the chime as Ivory put in the numbers, and then the automated pronouncement that the stay mode was on. Ivory turned on the kitchen light, and then more lights as she padded through, checking to make sure things were as she left them.

"Everything good," Roman asked, as he watched the house become more illuminated.

"Yes, everything is good."

"Excellent."

Ivory padded back to her bedroom. She had already kicked off her shoes in the kitchen and walked on tiptoe until she reached the carpeted space. She didn't like to sit on her bed in outside clothes, so instead, she sat down on a chaise lounge in front of it. She was waiting for Roman to say good night, or good morning, whatever the case may be. He didn't, though.

"Should I let you go," Roman asked. "I'm sure you're tired."

He wasn't. But he didn't have to go into the office in a few hours. Roman could work from wherever he was. That was the benefit of being his own boss and the CEO of his family's company. He had to be respectful of Ivory's time. Although being with Roman energized Ivory, she knew she had another long day ahead.

"I should probably try and get some rest."

"Sleep well, beloved."

"I'll talk to you soon," Ivory replied.

There was still a pause as Roman waited for Ivory to disconnect the call. Finally, realizing he wasn't going to end the call, Ivory did. And then she picked up her phone to give Roman a taste of his own polite medicine.

*Please text me when you get home safely.*

She smiled as she hit send. And Roman smiled when he received it.

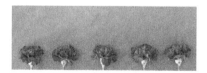

## Chapter Eleven

*I*vory placed the phone on the chaise and stood up, beginning to get undressed before she ascended to her full height. She had been in her work clothes longer than she cared to, and all she wanted was a hot shower and comfy pj's. By the time, Ivory made it to her adjoining bathroom, she was completely undressed. She felt the cool of the travertine floor under her feet as she walked to the glass shower. Reaching in, Ivory turned on the shower and while waiting for the water to warm, padded to the mirror to remove the little makeup she had on. Quickly, the mirror she used steamed over, and Ivory entered the shower, welcoming the warm water. She stood there, directly under the spray, allowing the steamy heat to wash the cares of the day away. The one thing that didn't was away was her thoughts of Roman.

As Ivory reached for the loofa and her scented body wash, her mind returned to her time with him; how much she laughed, how he smiled, how he made her feel. And that kiss?

Ivory's eyes rolled into the top of her head as her lips pursed slightly, reliving that special moment, so intensely, she could feel herself back in the security of Roman's arms as he ravenously kissed her soul.

"Shit," Ivory mumbled as her jewel convulsed at the thought. It was too much, the thought was too much, and Ivory stepped right in front of the shower head, allowing the heat to spray her face and run down the length of her. She needed to cool down internally. She hoped the hot shower would do it. By the time Ivory stepped out, her body had been pummeled by the heated jets. She realized just how physically exhausted she was. Grabbing a towel, Ivory wrapped her body in the cottony goodness and then wrapped another around her hair. With a third towel, Ivory wiped her arms and legs of the last remaining vestiges of the shower. Once dry, Ivory made her way back to the bedroom, her feet cushioned by the carpet. As she made her way to the walk-in closet, Ivory picked up her cellphone and swiped it to see if she had a message. She wasn't sure where Roman was staying or how long it would take him to get home, but she checked, nonetheless.

*I'm home safely and instantly missing you.*

And instantly, Ivory was smiling. She shook her head at how she was reacting. It was so unlike her. Ivory was a deep thinker, slow to get riled up, good or bad. She never let her guard down with men, especially on the 'first date'. But was this really a first date with Roman? She laughed and shook her head, making her way into the closet and retrieving pajamas from the dresser. She read the text again and found herself still smiling. Ivory decided to text back.

*Aw, that's so sweet.*

By the time she eased into her pj's and put the wet towels in the hamper, her phone chimed, indicating a new message.

*Because you are just that sweet to me.*

*Are you trying to make me blush,* Ivory texted back.

*Are you?* Roman quickly replied.

*Possibly* 😊

Ivory pulled back her duvet and climbed into bed, pulling the warm covers over her legs.

*Why aren't you asleep?* Ivory asked.

It didn't take long before another reply came through.

*Honestly, I can't stop thinking about you. I'm more concerned about you, though. You need your rest. The sun will be up in just a few hours.*

*I know,* Ivory replied, as she sunk down under the covers. *I'm going,* she replied.

*Good night, beautiful, or should I say, good morning.*

*Good morning.*

Ivory placed her phone on the nightstand by her bed and tried to settle in. She only had a few hours before her alarm clock would be sounding, telling her it was time to get up and do it all over again. She whispered a prayer and closed her eyes, steadying her breathing to try and rest. At some point, Ivory must have fallen asleep. But just as Roman occupied her thoughts while she was awake, he was there in her dreams too, blending reality from the dream world.

Roman wasn't fairing much better in the penthouse of the

W Hotel, downtown Atlanta. He knew sleep would allude him, so instead of laying in the bed, hoping sleep would find him, Roman poured a drink from the bar. Maybe the brandy would help to settle him. But his thoughts, just as her thoughts were completely occupied. Being reunited with Ivory was better than Roman could have ever imagined. But he wouldn't be satisfied with merely reuniting. Roman already knew, deep in his soul, that he wanted more... so much more. No woman past or present had ever made Roman feel the way Ivory did. She was easy to be around. There was no presumption and no presupposition. She knew him regular, not affluent, and accepted him just as he was. Roman could only hope that her new knowledge of him didn't change how she saw him, how she dealt with him. So far, it had gone okay. But who knows? Who knows when the reality of his reality truly set in with Ivory, would his wealth make a difference?

She wasn't shallow, not in the least bit, nor did he think Ivory was easily impressed. She dealt with dignitaries and international VIP's on a daily basis. Roman prayed that his VIP status didn't adversely affect what he hoped would be a new relationship. That's what he wanted, a real, adult relationship with the woman that stole his heart a long time ago. Roman took another long sip of the brandy, emptying the glass. The libation smoothly coated his throat and settled warmly in his stomach. Still, he wasn't sleepy. He didn't know if sleep would be possible, considering everything he was contemplating. Roman checked his watch and then crossed the penthouse and retrieved his laptop. There was one thing he knew he could do that would occupy him, not necessarily take thoughts of Ivory away but keep him from fixating on the possibilities.

Opening the computer, Roman poured another drink while he waited for the computer to power up. The international stock market was open. He could trade some stock and review a few of his investment portfolios until sleep overtook him. For Roman, it wasn't so much about making money. He had more money than he could spend in two lifetimes. Wheeling and dealing in the markets was all about calculated risk taking, and adventurous thrill seeking to see if his business intuitions would pay off. He loved researching a particular stock to trade and then critically thinking about the short-term and long-term possibilities for growth. And when he hit big, there was no greater thrill. More times than not, Roman would take the money he earned from a new investment that paid big dividends and donate it to a worthy cause. One of his favorite things to do was find a start-up company that he felt showed a great deal of promise and become a silent investor from monies he earned trading on international floors. There were times when the companies never knew who their benefactor was. The anonymity of blessing someone without his involvement being public kept his philanthropic efforts pure. Roman didn't do it for the accolades or the praise. He did it because he genuinely cared about people. He knew that there were far too many people, through no fault of their own, that suffered unnecessarily because of the lack of capital or the lack of support. Brilliant ideas excited him and Roman thrived off making brilliant ideas reality for entrepreneurs' young in the game, especially those that looked like him.

By the time Roman traded in multiple countries, in various markets, the sun was fully positioned in the sky. Trading invigorated him, and time moved by quickly without Roman even noticing. But now that he took a break, Roman realized that he hadn't even bothered to get undressed before he started working. Stretching his long arms overhead, Roman stood up from the desk and stretched again. Stepping from behind the desk, Roman began unbuttoning his shirt. By the time he reached the master, Roman's shirt was off, and he was unbuckling the Italian leather belt that held up his tailored slacks. Multiple jets greeted his muscular frame as he stepped into the blaring shower.

But the water didn't keep thoughts of Ivory from invading his thoughts. As the water pelted his body in all directions, Roman closed his eyes and was immediately back with her, holding her, kissing her, his body pressed up against hers. And just as it had before, his body responded to her; the scent of her, the way she felt in his arms. Roman's nature started to rise, thickly, solidly. The pressure was intense as his manhood swole hard. He had to relieve the pressure. Roman thought about Ivory as he stroked himself, his body still pelted by the warm water.

Remembering her lips pressed against his tightened his core as he could feel her lips, inhale her scent, feel the small of her back and the press of her thighs against him; the swell of her full breasts against his chest. Roman's stroke increased as he allowed the fantasy of Ivory to invade his mind, and his heart completely. He wanted her desperately, but not just physically. He wanted Ivory in totality. And Roman would not be satisfied until he had her.

WHEN THE ALARM CLOCK SOUNDED, IVORY DIDN'T immediately hear it. She rolled over and nestled further down in the comfort of her bed. Fortunate for her, she set more than one alarm just in case so the second time the irritating, yet familiar sound penetrated her dream space, Ivory had no choice but to answer the call.

"Uhn," she groaned, pulling the cover over her head instead of pulling it away. She didn't want to get up. The bed felt way too good to abandon it so quickly. But she knew she had to. Behind the kind of day, they had yesterday, there was a lot of paperwork and correspondence that had to be attended to. Diplomat Adebisi counted on Ivory to not only handle the translating, but also following up with many of the dignitaries they encountered as a part of their mission. With another heavy sigh, Ivory relinquished the warmth of her bed, peeling the covers from her body and swinging her legs over the side as she sat up. Once her feet hit the floor, there was no return to the bed, not until it was time to sleep again.

But in order to wake up fully, Ivory knew she needed a

quick shower to shock her system into wakefulness. This shower wasn't as long and luxurious as the night before. It wasn't intended to be. Ivory handled her business and exited just as quickly. With a towel wrapped around her, Ivory went through her morning routine, cleansing her face, and styling her hair. She applied a little mascara and a little concealer under her eyes and then exited the bathroom. Because she was a planner by nature, Ivory's clothes for the week were laid out in the closet. All she had to do was get dressed. By the time she exited the closet, Ivory was just about ready.

Grabbing her cell phone off the nightstand, and picking up earrings from her jewelry box, Ivory padded through the house to the kitchen. She wasn't much on caffeinated drinks, neither coffee nor pop, but this morning, Ivory knew she needed a little pick me up. Opening the refrigerator, she found a lone can of pop left over from the last time her sisters were at her house. It would have to do. Picking up her keys, briefcase, and purse, Ivory set the alarm and headed out the door. Once she was settled in the car, Ivory hit the garage door opener and started the ignition. The buzz of her phone drew Ivory's attention. She paused long enough to connect the cell phone to her car so she could continue. Ivory was looking over her shoulder as the phone line came to life.

"Are you alone?"

"What?" Ivory guffawed, clearing the garage and turning toward the console. Of course, she recognized the voice to be that of her kid sister.

"Why wouldn't I be alone," Ivory challenged. "What you trying to say about me?" Hitting the button to close the

CELESTE GRANGER

garage door, Ivory waited until the door was completely shut before putting the car in drive and moving down the street.

"You still didn't answer the question smart ass," Trinity teased.

"Why are you up so early any way," Ivory questioned.

"You're not the only one who has important work to do," Trinity scoffed.

"Right, sis," Ivory acquiesced.

"How in the hell did you run into Roman, Lil Rommie Rom?" Trinity asked. She was on her way into work as well, but there was no way she was going to wait to find out about what she saw the previous evening.

"It was a fluke," Ivory chuckled, "a total fluke."

"Or destiny," Trinity mused.

"Destiny?" Ivory rebuffed. "Girl, please."

"Don't discount it," Trinity corrected.

"And why not?"

"Because," Trinity continued. "You and Roman, I can see it."

"Really?"

"Yeah, really," Trinity answered. "Ivory, Roman was crazy about you back in the day. I don't know how you didn't see that."

Ivory's brow furrowed as she maneuvered the car onto the interstate on ramp. It felt like de ja vu, after hearing confirmation of the same thing from Roman the night before.

"He was my friend," Ivory said.

"Yeah, but anybody with eyes could see he wanted to be

112

more than that," Trinity countered. "Anyway, he didn't spend the night?"

"Oh, just cut to the chase why don't you," Ivory clapped back.

"It ain't like he's a stranger," Trinity laughed. "And he fine as hell now!"

"He is fine," Ivory agreed, laughing along with her sister.

"He was cute back in the day, but now? Huh, Roman is fine!" Trinity continued as the laughter died down. "I don't know why you didn't let him stay over, Ivory. It's been a while."

That was the problem with confiding in your sister and her knowing your business. They could bring it back to your remembrance. But Ivory didn't need a reminder of how long it had been since she was with someone intimately. Her body reminded her of that all too well the night before.

"That doesn't make me easy," Ivory insisted.

"Yeah," Trinity agreed. "But it does make you horny!"

When Trinity started laughing again, Ivory found herself laughing with her, at her own expense.

"Go straight to hell, Trin," Ivory quipped, "with gasoline drawers."

"Long as you get you some, I'll go," Trinity giggled.

"Get off my phone. Go to work. Do something with your life," Ivory playfully scolded.

"Love you, too," Trinity smiled. "Talk to you later."

# Chapter Twelve

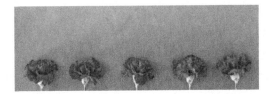

*I*vory was still smiling when the line disconnected. She and Trinity had always been close. Being the last two of eight daughters, and very close in age, the sisters were the best of friends. It just made sense. Because of that, Ivory and Trinity shared just about everything, and Trinity probably knew Ivory better than anyone. The fact that she made the same observation about Roman was interesting, and she mulled over it as she continued to drive into the office. If Roman's attraction was so obvious to other people, why didn't she see it? How could she have missed it?

Maybe because she didn't want to, Ivory mused. Knowing that Roman was interested in her in a romantic way would have certainly changed the nature of their earlier relationship. Ivory thought about it, all the time they spent together, how close they really were. It was nothing for Roman to be at her house, in her bedroom watching television or playing video games or doing absolutely nothing at all. Her parents trusted Roman enough to allow it. He had ingratiated himself into the family in such a way that everyone treated him like the brother they never had, and for her parents, like the son that alluded them after eight girls. Ivory remembered many times, Roman would hang out with her dad, doing guy stuff; watching football games, tinkering on the car, whatever men did when they were together. And Ivory's mother loved to have Roman over for dinner. He was always complimentary of her home cooking, and he always cleaned his plate. Roman didn't have to be told to help around the house after enjoying time with the Moore family. He would do the things the girls preferred not to do like take out the trash or rake the yard. There was never another young man who was allowed such access to their daughter.

Romantic inclinations from Roman West... Ivory was still thinking about it when she arrived at the embassy.

There was a lift in her step as Ivory strolled into the building. She'd been fortunate enough to land the job at the embassy after completing her master's degree in international business. The fact that Ivory spoke multiple languages was irresistible to a place like the embassy. Her skill set was in high demand, and she was assigned to Diplomat Adebisi two years ago. Ivory had been in awe of Fazilah's work in Sudan since she read about her in the news a year or so before. Adebisi's work was hard and important. Ivory was honored to be able to join in the fight to try and effect real change in South Sudan. The plight of those young women, although thousands of miles away, resembled similar struggles of young women in America. Too many were sexually exploited, unheard, and undervalued. Ivory hoped that what they were able to accomplish in Sudan would not only penetrate that continent but also make an impact in the US, eventually.

"Good morning," Ivory sang as she replied to the security guard's greeting. He smiled widely. The guard always thought the young lady who worked for the diplomat was beautiful, but today, she looked especially gorgeous. It was the smile she was wearing that made the difference. The guard still wore a smile on his lips long after Ivory was out of sight. Ivory didn't realize the impact she had on passerbys. She wasn't even cognizant of the fact that she was smiling herself.

"Good morning," Ivory greeted the executive assistant, Gwendolyn Smithton, as she entered the diplomat's suite.

"Good morning, Ms. Moore," Gwendolyn answered.

Ivory paused long enough at Gwen's desk to see if there were any messages for her. Gwen noticed there was a little something going on with Ms. Moore. Gwendolyn had worked for Fazilah about as long as Ivory, and they had a wonderful working relationship that sometimes spilled over into friendship. Ivory was mindlessly shimmying as she combed through the messages. Gwendolyn watched her for a minute, not saying anything, but she had to find out what it was that had Ms. Moore in such a good mood.

"Care to share," Gwen encouraged.

"Huh?" Ivory replied, being drawn out of her own daydream.

"Something's got you shimmying and shaking this morning," Gwendolyn teased. "Or is it someone? Maybe that fine specimen of a man that couldn't keep his eyes off you yesterday?"

"What?" Ivory immediately flushed. And then her brow furrowed as she wondered how Gwen would know. There was no doubt who the secretary was referencing; however, no doubt at all, at least not for Ivory. And then Ivory thought about it. Gwendolyn was in and out of the meeting yesterday on multiple occasions. She was also vicariously privy to the exchange between Roman and Fazilah. As Ivory was the right hand of the diplomat, Gwendolyn was the left hand, standing in close proximity during the greeting ceremony. That must have been how she witnessed the exchange between the two. That's what Ivory presupposed. But at this point, however she knew, Gwen knew. It was almost as bad as one of her sister's knowing. She wasn't going to let Ivory get away with anything.

"Ah, Mr. Roman West," Gwen playfully confirmed, as though she read the question on Ivory's mind. There was no point in trying to deny what Gwen said as the mention of his name dramatically increased the smile on Ivory's face and the rise of heat in her cheeks.

"I have no idea what you are talking about, Gwendolyn," Ivory replied much to officially.

"Okay, Missy ma'am," Gwendolyn teased, "but your face gives your whole game away."

Ivory tried to blow Gwen off with a careless toss of her hand, dismissing the comment as she walked away. Gwen knew better, though. Ivory had turned completely red in the face at the mere mention of Mr. West's name. Ivory made it to her office and put her things down. She needed to speak to the diplomat to double check the schedule for the day. That was important. There were always things that came up unexpectedly that would shatter Ivory's previously precisely made plans. If that was going to be the case today, Ivory wanted to know about it as early in the day as possible Who knows? She may have plans later that she wouldn't want to have ruined.

"Good morning, Diplomat Adebisi."

"Good morning, beloved," Fazilah smiled. She was still in the best mood because of how successful the engagement had gone the day before. The response from those in power had been more than she could have imagined. It had been a good day and gave Fazilah added hope that the impact she intended to make would be more significant, and sooner than she thought, she would be able to intervene before. Every day that went by where one more girl could be sold off into marriage or compromised in some way that made her want to die was one day too many. The funds that were raised during the event would provide a much-needed influx of money that could be used immediately to bolster the work happening on the ground.

"Did you rest well," Adebisi asked as Ivory settled down across the desk from her.

"It never seems like enough," Ivory replied, which was the safe response. She didn't know if Fazilah was continuing the inquiry Gwendolyn started or whether Fazilah's inquiry was from a pure space.

"And how about you, ma'am, did you sleep well?"

That was a good way to keep the conversation cordial

and on track, Ivory thought to herself as she got comfortable in the chair. She took out her digital pad that she took notes on during her meetings with the diplomat and prepared for the business of the day.

"Would you like to begin with the day's agenda," Ivory encouraged.

When Fazilah wasn't immediately responsive, Ivory looked up from her notepad to see what was going on. She saw Fazilah looking straight ahead, unfocused, with a faraway look in her eye. There was a smile that teetered at the corners of her lips, so whatever she was contemplating didn't seem to be negative. Ivory was patient, not wanting to preempt Fazilah's thought process. She could very well be considering their next move, their next event, the next action they would take to bring change to the girls back in Fazilah's home country.

"I still cannot believe the generosity of the donors on last evening," Fazilah mused aloud.

Ivory nodded her head in agreement but didn't say anything.

"With the help of special people, like dear Mr. Roman West, we'll be able to implement the next phase of our intervention months earlier than we thought," she continued. "Do you know how many girls we can possibly save because of their graciousness? How many girls won't have to spend another night in the home of a man two, three times her age, scared of what would happen next? How many families we can reach out to try and educate and possibly change their way of thinking. We can introduce a new means of trade, a new economic marker that doesn't include the pedaling of female flesh. I'm just," Fazilah paused as her eyes misted over once again, much like they had done the night before. "I'm just so full."

Diplomat Adebisi couldn't hold back the tears, and Ivory felt every bit of her passion and her pain. Emotion was so high in the room, it was palpable. Ivory, for the first time since their reintroduction, didn't have a physical response to hearing Roman's name again. The moment was much bigger than that. Fazilah wasn't just crying for the girls in South Sudan. She was crying from the pain of her past; a past that left her battered and bruised but thankfully didn't break her. The tears that she shed were for her past that continued to fuel her present-day passion. It grew harder for Ivory not to join in, feeling the sorrow and the hope deeply. She didn't say anything, though, and gave Fazilah the space she needed to grieve and to consider.

"Forgive me," the diplomat offered after a few moments.

"For what," Ivory sighed. "You have the right to feel however you feel," she reminded. "No forgiveness necessary."

"I appreciate that," Fazilah replied, offering a slight smile. She reached for a box of Kleenex sitting on her mahogany desk and after retrieving it, gently dabbed at the corners of her eyes.

"Okay," Fazilah smiled more fully. "Let's get to it, okay?"

With a nod of the head, Ivory was ready, and the ladies got right to work; not before Ivory quietly wiped the corners of her eyes just as fresh tears pressed to fall. They worked in tandem for three hours straight, reviewing the second phase of the educational component that would be introduced to the families in Sudan. Tribal leaders were often the most difficult to work with. Where the women in the tribes were far more receptive to what it is Fazilah had to say, the women were not in charge. They were not the ones in control, unfortunately. The all-male tribal leadership had been doing the things they had been doing for years; practices passed down from generation to generation, man to man, son to son. Trading young girls was a way of life, they were a commodity, and many tribal leaders felt like outside influences should not interfere in tribal matters. It was only because Fazilah was one of them that they even bent an ear out of respect to hear what it was she had to say. It was only because she was South Sudanese that they respected her enough to entertain her presence. But she was still a woman. She was a woman who allowed herself to be influenced by westernized culture, in tribal leader's estimation. She had forsaken tradition, abandoning the ways of her people. So, the leaders didn't welcome Diplomat Adebisi with open arms. It was a fight. It was a fight between the old and new. It was a patriarchal fight. It was a gender battle. It was war.

Although weary at times, Fazilah was not giving up the fight. She couldn't afford to. There were far too many girls depending on her to help. And there had been some progress made. Some women were breaking with tradition, breaking with their families at the risk of being disenfranchised, raising their voices, and refusing to go unheard. Any progress, any move in the right direction was good, and Fazilah and her supporters wanted to ensure that progress was not halted. The monies that had been donated were routed to those programmatic endeavors that would have the most immediate impact, and neither Fazilah nor Ivory stopped until every dollar was itemized and accounted for.

"Excuse me, ladies," Gwendolyn said after knocking on the door and being invited in.

"Yes," Diplomat Adebisi replied, lifting her head from her work.

"Sorry to disturb you, Madam Adebisi," Gwendolyn said, "but you have a special delivery."

"Oh, really," Fazilah exclaimed. "Come, let me see!"

For a brief moment, Gwendolyn disappeared, leaving the office door standing slightly ajar. When she returned, both of her hands were full.

"What do we have here," Fazilah exclaimed as Gwendolyn padded over to the desk.

Gwendolyn was smiling as she handed a gift bag to the diplomat and then turned and handed a long box to Ivory.

"For me," Ivory questioned, accepting the unexpected package.

"That's what the card says," Gwen answered, with a wink and a sly smile.

Standing to her feet, Fazilah placed the gift bag in the center of her desk.

"Now, what do we have here, huh," she chimed as she reached for the card attached.

Gwendolyn and Ivory waited as Fazilah read the card silently. After she was done, she clasped her hands together near her heart, and the women watched as a smile spread across Fazilah's beautiful face.

"He is too kind," Fazilah sighed, "just too kind."

With a deep sigh, the diplomat reached into the gift bag and lifted the protective tissue that covered her gift.

"Oh my, no," Fazilah gasped, reaching into the bag.

Ivory and Gwendolyn were just as excited to see what had the diplomat so thrilled.

"How?" She asked rhetorically as she lifted a potted plant from inside the bag. She wore a brilliant smile and could tell by the looks on the girls' faces that they had no idea why she was so overjoyed.

"This is oeceloclades maculate," Fazilah declared as if that information was somehow enlightening. Ivory and Gwen could appreciate the beauty of the plant with its brightly spotted blooms and Kelly-green leaves. But that was about it.

"This is the monk orchid," Fazilah explained, "a plant native to my country. That he would take the time to determine what was true to my culture says a lot about the kind of man he is. As if the generous donation he made wasn't enough, uhn? Mr. West is a thoughtful man, a thoughtful, thoughtful man. And this incredible gift, this reminder of home, warms my heart."

This time when Ivory heard Roman's name, she felt her heart beat a little bit faster.

"I take it Mr. West sent you something too, eh, Ivory?" Fazilah asked.

"I guess," Ivory replied, doing her best not to blush. Her reaction wasn't conscious. She didn't choose to feel butterflies in her stomach at the mere mention of Roman's name or have her cheeks filled with hot heat when she thought about him. In fact, Ivory didn't fully understand why she was feeling her body manifested such a physical reaction and made her feel so giddy about a boy, now man that had always been her best friend.

There was a knowing look shared between the diplomat and the secretary that drew Ivory's attention away from her own subconscious thoughts.

"What's that all about?" Ivory dared to question. Her eyes darted between the two women, looking to see who was going to give it up first.

A broad smile danced on the lips of the diplomat. And when she laughed, clapping her hands at the same time, Ivory knew there was something to their exchange.

"Let's see what Mr. West has for you, uhn? Then you can raise your question again."

Gwendolyn's nod of agreement didn't make the teasing tension in the room any better.

"Come on, Ms. Moore," Gwen added. "Let's see."

"Read the card first, uhn, Ivory," Fazilah encouraged, still wearing too wide a smile.

"Out loud," Gwen taunted, smiling herself.

"You didn't," Ivory reminded.

"Yes, that is true, but you should," Fazilah replied.

"That is so not fair," Ivory said, taking the card from the glossy white box and opening the envelope. She pre-read the note, and instantly her cheeks flushed with warm color.

"Uhn," Fazilah sighed. "It must be something good."

When Ivory hesitated like she had no intention of sharing, Gwendolyn moved towards her, peering over Ivory's shoulder, trying to sneak a peek.

"Uhn uhn," Ivory chided, pressing the card to her chest to keep Gwen from seeing it.

"It must be good," Gwen smirked.

Ivory didn't lift the card from her chest fast enough, and the eyes of the two ladies bore into her with a challenge in their brow.

"Fine," she acquiesced. "I'll read it."

It was only when she lifted the card and began to read it did the women look satisfied. Ivory was so embarrassed, but she pressed on, knowing that the fallout would be at her expense.

*Although a dozen roses are what most people give, I am not most people, and neither are you. There is one rose for every year that I have known you, cherished you, and loved you.*

She didn't look up right away as she heard sounds of swooning women all around her.

"Ahnn," Fazilah squealed.

"Your card didn't say that, did it, Fazilah," Gwen sighed.

"No, no, it didn't," Fazilah chimed. "Nothing like that."

Ivory still didn't look up. She could feel the heat in her cheeks and the warmth that descended to her heart. Roman's sentiment was very heartfelt and required some explaining if she was going to get Fazilah and Gwen off her case.

"He didn't mean it like that," Ivory defended.

"Like what?" Fazilah lovingly challenged. "Like he has a fondness for you? Like he cares about you?"

"Like friends," Ivory explained. "He meant it like we're friends."

"I don't know, Ms. Fazilah," Gwen mused, folding her

125

arms across her ample chest and leaning into her hip. "Sounds like Mr. West wants to be more than just friends."

"I think so," Fazilah agreed.

"Nah," Ivory dismissed, ignoring the pounding of her heart.

"Would that be such a bad thing?" Fazilah asked.

"He is a fine man, Ms. Ivory," Gwen added. "In more than one way!"

"Uhn hun," Fazilah grinned.

"Diplomat," Ivory challenged.

"He is," Fazilah giggled. "There is no denying that!"

"You too are a whole mess," Ivory laughed.

The three were all smiles and laughs as Ivory finally opened the box.

"Ah, those are beautiful," Gwen sighed, as Ivory revealed the gorgeously brilliant red roses sprinkled with baby's breath inside.

"I'll take care of those for you," Gwen continued. Ivory saw that Gwen held her hand over her heart like she was moved by Roman's gesture.

"Thank you," Ivory replied, briefly lifting the box to her nose and inhaling the aromatic scent before handing the flowers to the secretary.

Once Gwen left the room, Ivory turned her attention back to the diplomat.

"Any other business we need to handle before the weekend?"

"You are very quick to get back to business, Ms. Ivory," Fazilah contemplated, steepling her hands under her chin. "That is very telling, beloved. Very telling indeed."

Although Fazilah wasn't much older than Ivory, her experiences made her seem so. She was wise beyond her years while still managing to hold on to a part of herself most people didn't have the opportunity to see. She was fun and funny and could be just as girly as the next. Fazilah let it go for the moment, but Ivory knew all too well that the conversation about Roman West was far from over. Ivory knew she had no choice but to accept it.

"Nothing else then," she quipped," stopping Fazilah short.

"Just one more thing," Fazilah replied as she closed the notebook on her desk and sat back contemplatively. "Don't be like me."

The abruptness of Fazilah's statement caught Ivory off guard. But before she could ask, the diplomat went on to explain.

"I have let my past dictate my present when it comes to matters of the heart," Fazilah sighed. "I may very well have let the one meant for me get away because I couldn't get past what I've been through. He tried desperately to convince me that I was worthy of love and that he was the man who could love me the right way. I couldn't hear it or see it. No matter what he did to try and convince me, I dismissed it and kept him at a distance; in a place, he didn't want to be. But I kept him there because I thought it was best. That I would be safe and protected by not exposing my heart to another soul. I refused to allow myself the possibility that real love was an option for me. Don't do that because it can cost you dearly in the end. It cost me, and I don't know if there will ever be another who could love me through my pain."

Fazilah paused as she reflected on her circumstance.

"Be open and receptive to what the universe has to offer. You never know. There could be more than friendship, and maybe even true love."

There was no need for any further commentary. Fazilah had spoken. It was up to Ivory to listen or leave it alone.

# Chapter Thirteen

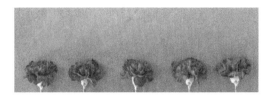

*T*hank you.

The text message Roman received was simple enough. Still, receiving it made him smile.

*Always.*

It wasn't anything new for Roman to try and put a smile on Ivory's face. Even when they were younger, he would do whatever he could to make her smile. But to make Ivory laugh was even better. The nice things he did generated the smile. He would clown, though. Cracking jokes, although he wasn't naturally funny or making a complete and total ass of himself just to see Ivory's face light up. No matter how silly he looked, when Roman got the result he wanted and her laughter filled the atmosphere, it was worth it.

But the next text lit his face up as well.

*I'm done for the day,* Ivory texted as she finally sat down behind the desk in her office.

Ever since they parted ways the night before, Roman

couldn't wait to see Ivory again. Sometimes you don't realize how much you miss a person until you have a chance to see them again. Seeing Ivory, having the opportunity to spend time with her, made Roman anxious to see her again. It didn't matter what they did. He just wanted to be with her.

*Plans?* He texted back. When he sent the message, Roman intended for it to be funny; a tease of sorts since he shared with Ivory the night before that he wanted to spend time with her. Although he hoped her answer would align with his desire, Roman couldn't help but feel a little trepidatious as he waited for her reply.

He didn't know that Ivory was smiling on the other end of the phone. She remembered what he said, yet, Ivory couldn't overlook a chance to make Roman squirm a little. He could be so cocky sometimes.

*Maybe...*

When Roman read it, he threw his head back and laughed heartily. Although the text was cryptic, her comment was refreshing, and he took it just like Ivory meant it. That was one of the things that he liked about dealing with her. She wasn't easily impressed, no matter what, and she didn't pull any punches when it came to putting him in check. Other women Roman encountered were too enamored with him. They weren't challenging, and too quick to agree because they wanted to please him no matter what. That was so not Ivory Moore.

With a chuckle still on his lips, Roman texted back.

*There's no maybe. I'll pick you up at eight.*

This time, Ivory was the one throwing her head back

with laughter. "That was a good one," she muttered as she considered her reply.

There was no doubt that she wanted to see Roman again. He was a good friend, after all. However, that wasn't the space Ivory operated from. Thinking about everything that happened the night before and the powerful words Fazilah shared, Ivory found herself seriously contemplating just what Roman could mean to her, and not just what he meant in the past.

*Don't get ahead of yourself, girl*, that cautionary voice sounded in her head.

*Whateva...* she decided to send back.

When his phone chimed, Roman swiped to see her smart-ass reply. He knew there would be one.

And just as he suspected, Ivory lived up to his expectations.

This time when he read it, Roman didn't laugh. Instead, he nodded his head with narrowed eyes and a smirk replacing his smile. He had something for her whatever. And Ivory would soon find out what that something was.

*Wear something comfortable*, he replied.

Now she would be the one wondering what he had up his sleeve.

*Ah shit*, Ivory hummed, seeing what Roman had to say. Grabbing her purse, Ivory stood up from her desk and padded towards the door. She wondered what he had in store. Admittedly, she was excited.

"Don't forget your flowers," Gwen called out as she saw Ivory passing by.

"Thanks, Gwen," Ivory replied, doubling back. "I sure would have."

She was preoccupied and rightfully so. After wishing the girls a good weekend, Ivory made her way out of the diplomat's suite and down the main corridor. She was grateful for the weekend after an exhausting week of work. The security guard was still there and gave Ivory as hearty a salutation as he did before. He watched as she exited the building, and once again, seeing her put a smile on his face. It was just after four p.m., and Ivory had a decision to make. She hadn't seen Kennedy and the baby in a few days, and she desperately wanted to check on her sister and hold her nephew again. Yet, she would love to go home, relax for a while and prepare for her time with Roman, not knowing what he had in store for her.

Ivory knew she needed to decide quickly, whatever her decision was going to be. By the time she made her way to her car, parked in the covered garage, Ivory had made her decision. It was family over everything. She needed to see Little Man Cecil.

By the time she arrived at Kennedy and Bryce's place, she was more than excited to see the family. Exiting her car, Ivory traipsed up the walkway to the front door. She thought about ringing the doorbell but opted against it, just in case the baby was sleeping. Instead, she gently rapped on the door, hoping someone inside would hear her. It didn't take long for the door to be answered.

"Hey, mom," Ivory replied with wide eyes, surprised to see her mother open the door.

"Shhh," Felicia cautioned with a smile. She reached out

and hugged her daughter and then stepped back so Ivory could cross the threshold. "Hey baby, good to see you," Felicia said, just above a whisper, closing the door behind them. "The little one is napping."

"Should I come back?"

"Oh, no," Felicia smiled. "Kennedy would love to see you."

"Are you sure," Ivory questioned. She hadn't even considered calling before showing up. Now, her visit with Ken and the baby could be in jeopardy. She didn't want to be completely selfish, but she was desperate for some baby time.

"I'm sure," Felicia reassured. "Come on," Felicia encouraged, taking the first step to the second floor.

Ivory kicked off her shoes and followed behind her mother, who was already bare foot. It was a practice in the Moore family not to wear outside shoes inside the house, not dragging in the world's woes into the sanctity of the home. By the time they reached the upper floor, Ivory was walking on tiptoe, trying desperately to keep quiet so as not to disturb the baby. They rounded the corner and made their way to the master bedroom. The door was cracked, and quietly, Felicia pushed it open.

"Is it okay if we come in," she asked, widening the opening so Kennedy could see her younger sister.

"Yes," Kennedy exclaimed in a loud whisper. "Come in," she encouraged, waving her hand and smiling.

Ivory was happy to see her sister and moved towards the bed. Leaning over, she wrapped her arms around Kennedy's neck and hugged her tightly. Ken returned the hug and then patted the side of the bed, encouraging Ivory to climb in. Kennedy didn't have to ask Ivory twice. The sisters, all the sisters were close, and climbing in the bed and cuddling up next to her big sister instantly made Ivory nostalgic.

"Mommy's been here the whole time?" Ivory asked, snuggling in next to her sister.

"Yes, and it has been so awesome," Kennedy sighed.

"She may never leave," Ivory teased.

"That's fine with me," Kennedy replied. "Her being here has helped so much."

"Bryce might not like that," Ivory playfully cautioned.

"Girl, please," Ken insisted. "He's enjoying her being here just as much as me; homecooked meals, a clean house, and she gets up with the baby in the middle of the night. Mom is a Godsend."

"How're you feeling, Ken," Ivory asked, wrapping her arm around her sisters.

"Exhausted," Ken exhaled. Her answer defied her aura, and Ivory leaned in, cuddling closer to her sister. "Blessed, happy and tired as hell," she huffed as a smile began to crease her lips. Kennedy had never been happier, and although she was tired, her heart and soul were elated.

Despite what Kennedy said, Ivory couldn't help but notice that Kennedy's pregnancy glow remained intact. And then she realized something that she had to bring to her sister's attention. Ivory gently pushed out her arm, bumping into Kennedy's swollen breast.

"The girls are so much bigger than before," Ivory whispered.

"Girl," Kennedy exhaled. "People tell you a lot of things

when you're pregnant and about to have a baby. Good or bad, people love to share, right? But nobody told me about this," Kennedy said, pointing at her mountainous breasts. "Sis, when my milk came in? Oh, my God! It was," she paused. "I don't even know how to describe it." Kennedy chuckled as she continued. "It was like when Moses waved his walking stick over the Red Sea, and the water came rushing back into place!"

"Wow," Ivory sighed. "I can't even imagine."

"No, you can't, I swear," Kennedy laughed louder than she expected and then shushed herself to try and keep from waking the baby. "And your nephew? Chile, he can eat!"

Ivory hid her giggle behind her hand.

"He eats for 45 minutes and sleeps for 15 and then eats again," Ken smiled, shaking her head. "Got me feeling like a dairy cow, I swear."

By this time, both sisters were cracking up. Just then, they heard rustling in the bassinet, and then the baby started to whimper.

"I'll get him," Ivory said anxiously, quickly scooting off the bed before Kennedy had a chance to object. Ivory was already grinning from ear to ear even before she reached the baby. When she leaned over the bassinet and saw him kicking his legs, stretching and yawning, the smile on Ivory's face grew exponentially.

"Hey, little man," she beamed, carefully reaching in and picking him up. Little Cecil continued to stretch and squirm as Ivory carefully tucked him in her arms, being careful to support his head.

"It's your favorite auntie, Ivory," she whispered as she

lifted him close to her face, inhaling his baby scent and kissing him lightly on the forehead. Ivory swore Cecil smiled at her behind the kiss, and she was giddy about it. She pivoted on her heels and faced her sister, wearing the goofiest grin.

"He's so precious, Ken."

"He is."

Ivory was careful as she crossed the bedroom. She eased back into the bed and adjusted the cap Cecil wore. She couldn't stop staring at him; taking in all his features and enjoying how he felt in her arms. Cecil rustled again, opening and closing his mouth. He turned his head towards Ivory and started rooting. Her eyes widened, and her mouth fell open as the baby nuzzled against her.

"I think he's hungry," Ivory chimed.

"Of course, he is," Kennedy replied, shaking her head.

"Come here, baba," she cooed as she reached for her son. The sisters were careful with the exchange of the infant, and once Cecil was successfully in his mother's arms, Ivory missed having him in hers. In his mothers' arms, Cecil became even more active, whimpering and nuzzling trying to find nourishment. Kennedy couldn't respond fast enough. Finally, Cecil latched on and was instantly comforted. Ivory watched in awe as his little hands cupped his mother's breasts and he was fed.

"Wow," Ivory mused, resting her head on her sister's shoulder and sharing the special moment with them.

"Amazing, isn't it," Kennedy replied. Ivory nodded her head in agreement.

"All of this, giving birth to this little wonder and being

able to nourish him with my own body completely reminds me of just how powerfully incredible we are as women, how much we give and how much we can give, and how fully we love. I have never been in love like this before, Ivory," Kennedy sighed as she cradled her son. "Never. I love Bryce with all my heart; don't get me wrong. But this one right here, he has my soul."

# Chapter Fourteen

*I*vory spent as much time as she could with Cecil and Kennedy. It was wonderful, and Ivory loved every minute of it. She felt different when she left and thought a lot about the things her sister shared with her about motherhood; the challenges, and the rewards. Ken seemed completely happy, like having a baby made her whole in some ways. There was a fullness to her life she hadn't known before her son was born. That seemed unphathomable to Ivory considering she knew how happy Kennedy was with Bryce. Cecil helped her to ascend to an even higher level of happiness.

*Wow* is all Ivory could think as she traveled the short distance to her home. Thinking about her sister's journey inevitably reminded Ivory of the absences in her own. She'd never had baby fever before, ever. But there was something about watching Kennedy with her son, and even holding Cecil herself that caused a different kind of swoon, a different kind of stirring for her. She was still full and thoughtful as she entered the house. Time had gotten away from Ivory, and it was nearly 7:00 o'clock p.m. Good thing Roman said dress comfortably. Even with that, Ivory knew she would have to hurry to be ready in time, especially since she had no idea what to wear.

Ivory started stripping at the door. By the time she made it to her bedroom, she was naked.

"What the hell am I going to put on," she mused aloud as she turned on the shower and stepped inside. One would think comfortable would be easy, but it wasn't. Ivory didn't want to be too comfortable that she wasn't presentable. At the same time, it was easy to be overdressed, particularly since she had no idea what Roman had planned.

*I should have asked,* Ivory fussed as she rinsed the last of the soapy water from her body and turned off the shower. Drying off and then wrapping the towel around her, Ivory took the time to moisturize her body with a mixture of essential oils especially designed for her. She hustled to the closet to figure out what to put on. Nothing seemed right as she combed her clothing selection. She held up a few outfits and wasn't satisfied with anything. Stepping out of the closet and peeking around the corner, she looked at the clock. It was already 7:30.

"Yikes!"

Ivory had to hurry. She ducked back into the closet. It was decision time. After a few moments, at least Ivory narrowed it down between two outfits; a pair of jeans that hugged her curves just right or a simple black dress that could be dressed up or down.

"When all else fails," Ivory hummed as she made her selection. Thankfully, it only took her a few minutes to slide on her little black dress. Ivory made her way to her makeup table and sat down. She didn't wear a lot, but makeup tables had the best lighting. After applying a bit of mascara and some gloss on her lips, Ivory had one more decision to make. Gold or silver?

Just then, Ivory heard her doorbell chime.

*Shit!*

Still barefooted, Ivory tiptoed towards the front door.

"Just a minute," she called out, which made her chuckle. She sounded like her Grand making her way to greet a guest. With a quick look in the hallway mirror, Ivory checked herself before opening the door. Fluffing her curly fro, Ivory turned and unlocked the door.

"Hey," Ivory said as Roman came into view, his six-foot-two-inch frame leaning against the doorjamb. He'd always been an attractive man. But as Ivory's eyes traveled the length of him, her mink lashes fluttering against her cocoa brown skin, she noticed just how handsome he really was. It was still odd having to look up at Roman, and as their eyes met again, he smiled.

"Hey," he replied. As Ivory's eyes took him in, he watched her, taking her fullness in as well. She was beautiful, naturally. And when she smiled, Roman felt it in his soul. Roman lifted his frame from the doorjamb and extended his arms, inviting Ivory in for a hug. She accepted, melding into him as she wrapped her arms around his waist. The curls of her crown tickled Roman's chin, and he leaned in, pulling her in closer. Ivory felt the strength of his muscular chest rise and fall against her cheek as she inhaled Roman's masculine scent. As they parted, Roman waited until Ivory invited him in before stepping over the threshold into her place.

"I'll be ready in just a minute," Ivory said. "Make yourself comfortable."

As Ivory disappeared down the hallway, casting a smile over her shoulder, Roman stepped out of his loafers before moving any further into her home. He'd been at the Moore family home plenty enough times to know their customs. It was one he adopted himself in his own space. Roman made his way into the living area, observing Ivory's style. It suited her; the pops of rich, bold color against a neutral backdrop reflected Ivory's aesthetic. As he approached the stone fireplace, Roman paused, looking at the pictures she had placed there. He saw familiar faces; faces of people he knew very well. There was an incredible picture of Ivory with her father, Cecil. Roman picked up the sterling silver frame and took a closer look. The picture captured Ivory looking up at her dad as he looked towards the camera. The photograph captured the way Ivory felt about her father. You could see the respect and love in her eyes.

"Are you ready?"

Hearing her voice caused Roman to pivot and turn towards her. Once again, he was entranced by just how amazing she looked. The off the shoulder black dress Ivory wore was like a second skin, accentuating the swell of her breast and the slender of her waist before grazing the rise of her full hips. The dress then fell away, leaving more to the imagination stopping just below her thighs. Although Ivory was smiling playfully, Roman's hooded eyes drank her in like fine wine.

"Will this work," Ivory asked, twirling on her pedicured toes, holding her stilettos with her manicured fingers.

"Absolutely," Roman crooned, folding in his lower lip and slowly releasing it. He wasn't trying to seduce her with his eyes. Roman was just mesmerized with how incredibly gorgeous Ivory was. She was pretty as a girl, but as a woman, Ivory was so much more exquisite. Roman's stride took him to the entryway where Ivory stood. He saw her balancing on the table to put her shoes on.

"Let me help," Roman offered.

"I've got it," Ivory replied, expressing her independence, exaggerating the furrow in her brow.

Roman stood close, looming over her. She had to look up to meet his eyes.

"Let me help you, beloved," Roman reiterated. His gaze was compelling yet kind. He wasn't trying to undermine her ability to take care of herself, and Ivory saw that resonate in the way he looked at her. She acquiesced, handing over her shoes to him. Roman dropped down to one knee and encouraged Ivory to place her hand on his shoulder for balance as he lifted one foot and then the other, gently placing the stilettos on her feet. When he was done, Ivory extended her delicate hand to help him up. Roman looked up and saw her offering. Although he could get up on his own, he appreciated Ivory's reciprocity and accepted her hand. Roman made sure to balance the majority of his weight on his legs as he stood to his full height.

"Thank you," she smiled with her eyes.

"Thank you."

Ivory turned and picked up her keys and her clutch.

"Ready?"

"Absolutely."

Roman slipped back on his Italian loafers and stepped back across the threshold so Ivory could close the door. He waited until it was locked before turning toward the walkway. Sliding her keys into her bag, Ivory joined Roman on the path to his vehicle. He walked slightly behind her, and she felt the strength of his hand to the center of her back. He guided and guarded her six. As they made their way to the car, Ivory noticed that this time, there was no driver. Activating the key fob, the black on black Maserati Levante came to life, and Roman escorted Ivory to the passenger side, making sure she was securely inside before closing the door and making his way to the driver's side. She waited until Roman was settled in before raising the question.

"So, what do you have planned?"

A smirk creased Roman's lips as he turned on the ignition, and the Maserati began to purr. Before answering, Roman turned to Ivory and reached across her, securing her seatbelt. His proximity was close, and Ivory inhaled his masculinity once again. Although she wanted to keep things light, her inhale didn't outweigh the escalated beat of her heart. Roman didn't immediately pull back as his proximity to her immediately aroused his aura as it had done every time he had the pleasure of being in Ivory's presence.

"It's a surprise," Roman crooned and then reluctantly eased away from her.

"Hmph," Ivory huffed. "Did you forget?"

"Forget what," Roman asked, wearing too wide a smile.

"That I hate surprises," Ivory insisted as she folded her arms across her chest.

"Hate is such a strong word," Roman replied, but the smile he wore didn't fade. He knew she was not one to be surprised, yet, that was the fun of it. He had to aggravate her a little, just for old times' sake.

"It might be a strong word," Ivory continued, not missing the glint in Roman's eyes. "Would you like me to rephrase?" She quipped.

"Can you," Roman teased.

"Do not test my gangster, Roman," Ivory chided. "I can rephrase in at least four languages."

A smirk turned up the corner of Roman's sexy lips, and he cut his eyes in her direction. Of course, Ivory took that as a challenge.

"Je deteste les surprises," she quipped in French.

"Ukrih almufajat," she enunciated in Arabic. "Huh?" She challenged, wearing a smirk.

"Odio las sorpresas," she rattled off in Spanish.

"Ha!" Roman exclaimed. "I ain't gone test you," he chortled, lifting his hand for Ivory to give him a high five. When she didn't, he turned slightly in her direction, gaining her eyes.

"You gone leave me hanging?"

"I should," Ivory countered. When Roman playfully pushed his hand forward three of four times, encouraging Ivory to give him some dap, she couldn't hold in the laugh that had been bubbling in her gut.

"Nnhnn," she mumbled, finally slapping his hand. He loved her feistiness and joined in when Ivory laughed again.

Roman loved the sound of Ivory's happiness, and as they moved through the Atlanta streets toward their destination, Roman kept Ivory laughing no matter how hard she fought against it.

"No way," Ivory declared, leaning up in the seat to make sure she got a good look.

"Yes, way," Roman teased as he parked the vehicle on the deserted lot.

"But it's closed," Ivory sighed as she eyed the door.

"Not for us."

# Chapter Fifteen

*R*oman couldn't put the car in park fast enough. The fact that Ivory seemed excited, heightened his emotional state. Turning off the ignition, Roman popped the trunk and then exited the SUV, quickly rounding the back of it to open Ivory's door. She accepted his extended hand and lifted her frame from the vehicle.

Once out of the car, Ivory stood there for a moment, relishing the notion that the skating rink that they frequented in their youth that had been closed for years was a possibility. Memories flooded back of how much fun they had back in the day. Cascade Skating Rink was the highlight of every weekend, from picking out the perfect outfit, to making sure your skates were polished and ready, to rolling out to all the latest jams. Just the thought put a smile on Ivory's face.

When she turned to face Roman, he was smiling too, as though he experienced her memories in the same way.

"You ready?"

"Uh, yeah, I guess," Ivory said, looking down at her outfit and the stilettos she wore.

Roman's eyes traveled the same way Ivory's did.

"Now, you know I'm not going to leave you hanging, right?"

Ivory shrugged her shoulders. This time, she was testing Roman's gangster, and he took her lifted shoulders as a challenge. With a slight pivot, Roman stride took him to the trunk of the car. Ivory couldn't see what he was doing and leaned forward to get a look. Still, she didn't see anything. When the trunk closed, Roman had a gift-wrapped package in his hand.

"Is that for me?"

"Of course," Roman affirmed, lifting his arm, bent at the elbow. She didn't fuss about this being yet another surprise. Roman was hardheaded, had always been. Ivory knew the more she made a fuss about it, the more he would do it, just to get her riled up. Instead of fussing, Ivory fell into place, easing her arm around Roman's as they walked stride for stride to the rink's entrance. Roman rapped lightly on the door, and within seconds, it was opened for them.

"Hey, my man," the owner, Sylvester Owens, said as he greeted Roman.

"Hey, bro," Roman replied, shifting the box in his hand to shake hands with Sylvester.

The owner greeted Ivory as well, and the two crossed the threshold together. It was like literally stepping back in time. Not much had changed inside the rink, and that was more than Ivory could hope for. Throwback music was already blasting through the speakers and the rotating disco lights that threw color around the room were already in full motion. Immediately, Ivory felt like dancing. Being back at the rink, after all this time, gave her just that kind of good feeling.

"Don't worry about getting the keys back to me, Sylvester said as he prepared to walk out the door, "I'll get them from you later."

"Thanks again, man," Roman said as he and Sylvester gave each other one final dap. "I appreciate you."

Sylvester was thoughtful enough to give Ivory a parting salutation before leaving. Ivory offered a smile and a casual wave as she continued to rock and sway to the old school beat. Rome refocused his attention back to Ivory as Sylvester locked the door on his way out.

"It looks like you're ready," Roman crooned, easing up beside her and slipping his free arm around her waist. Ivory continued to sway as she looked up into his eyes.

"This is so good, Roman," Ivory swooned. "I can't believe you did this!"

Roman, still holding on to her, turned slightly stepping in front of Ivory.

"Why not?" He asked.

She knew it was a loaded question, and the flush in her cheeks let Roman know she knew. From as long as Ivory could remember, Roman had always done things for her; things even her boyfriends at the time, wouldn't do. Whether it was staying up all night with her and helping her study for a big test; fighting battles Ivory didn't want to fight, or surprising her with the little things that always managed to put a smile on her face. He was thoughtful, considerate, and had always been. Roman seemed to get just as much satisfaction out of making her happy as if he'd done something for himself. Back then, Ivory didn't always put it together just how much Roman showed he cared, but with this gesture, those memories came flooding back, washing over her and filling Ivory with the kind of warm and fuzzy feelings that warmed her internally. All those little things combined with the things Ivory recently learned about Roman cast new light on how she saw his 'kind' gestures. The warm and fuzzies were tinged with new feeling; an adult feeling that Ivory couldn't deny.

There was no need for Ivory to offer a verbal response. The look in her eyes was enough for Roman.

"Come on," he encouraged as he stepped to her side. Roman encouraged Ivory's movement, not just with his words but with his body. She felt him move next to her, and the natural inclination to move with him came easy. As the music continued to play in the background, Roman escorted Ivory to the benches that lined the rink and suggested she sit down. She complied, with a puzzled look on her face, especially when he knelt down in front of her with the gift box in his hand.

"What are you doing," Ivory mused with an undeniable smile on her face, more nervous than flattered. This position, Roman kneeling in front of her, made Ivory's heart pound in her chest even though she knew he wasn't proposing. A wave of nausea settled in her belly, and suddenly, Ivory felt like she couldn't quite catch her breath.

"Just hold on a second," Roman smiled. He loved to see

her feign disgust while still being excited underneath. Roman extended the box so Ivory could pull the bow. She shook her head but pulled the ribbon, nonetheless. Once the ribbon slid from the box, Roman sat it down next to him and took the top off, revealing matching tissue paper that hid Ivory's gift from her. He lifted the box to her again. Ivory was reluctant. The shape of the box gave nothing away, and the slight smile that curled the corners of Roman's full lips only told Ivory that he was enjoying the suspense way too much. Slowly, Ivory lifted her hand and eased the tissue paper back. Instantly her eyes widened, and then she covered her face with both hands.

"No way!" Ivory exclaimed as she revealed her face. She cradled her chin in her hands and uttered the words again. "No fuckin' way."

"I hope that means you like it," Roman teased. Her answer to his question was clear, but he couldn't resist rubbing it in. Ivory claimed she didn't like surprises, but he was two for two so far. Roman watched as the realization of what he held in his hands registered on Ivory's face.

"And with the pom pom's and everything?!?"

She was flabbergasted. Roman somehow managed to surprise her with her old rolling skates, the ones she wore every Saturday when they were younger but hadn't seen in years.

"You called my mom?" Ivory laughed. It was as much a statement as a question. That's where her skates had been at her parent's home. Ivory laughed as she shook her head. He went through a great deal of thoughtful effort with this surprise. It warmed her heart in a way Roman couldn't even imagine. Ivory couldn't stop smiling; she really couldn't. Roman sprang into action, knowing she was pleased. He eased one stiletto then the other from Ivory's feet, making sure to rest her heels on his thighs instead of the rink floor. Reaching into the box, Roman pulled out a thick pair of socks for her to wear and then eased them onto each foot, straightening them and handling Ivory with care. Once finished, Roman was careful to help Ivory with her skates, making sure they were comfortable before he stood up.

"You good?"

"So good," she smiled.

Roman's preparation showed as he sat down next to her, pulling his old skates from under the bench. Ivory was still stunned at just how thorough he had been in trying to please her. With his skates on, Roman seemed like a giant as Ivory peered up the length of him from her seated position. With ease, he stepped in front of her and extended both his hands to help Ivory to standing.

"Be careful now," Roman warned. "It's been a while."

"Oh, you got jokes, huh?" She teased as she stood in front of him. Ivory slid her hands up her ample hips and rested them there to emphasize her point. Roman was so distracted by her sexy move; he was slow in responding. She watched him watching her and playfully pushed Roman against his brick-hard chest.

"You make me so sick," Ivory hummed as she took the first few steps towards the rink from the carpeted floor. Roman didn't stop watching as he pivoted on his skates to watch her move in front of him. Womanhood had been good to Ivory, and Roman appreciated her feminine curves.

She was not to be played with. His inference that she might be rusty on her wheels was fuel for Ivory. After a careful step onto the slick rink, Ivory started feeling herself. Skating was just like riding a bike. It didn't take long for it to come back to her. She moved smoothly, and when the beat dropped for "No Diggity," Ivory dipped low in her hips and rocked sexily from side to side. Spinning around and stopping in reverse, she faced Roman and enticed him to meet her on the floor. Roman's eyes tightened, and he folded in his lower lip releasing it slowly watching Ivory dance in front of him. Her fingers called to him, but it was the curve of Ivory's smile that compelled his feet to move.

Roman had always been smooth, and when he stepped out onto the rink, nothing had changed, except the length of his glide. He and Ivory were infamous for their partner skating back in the day. When he wrapped his arm around her waist this time, yeah, something had changed. She no longer looked down to meet his eyes, and the hold he had on her waist was no longer friendly. Roman tucked her in comfortably, yet possessively against him although they were the only two people in the space. Ivory didn't mind at all as they glided in sync to the rhythmic beats. Every time a new song dropped; it was a flashback to their times together before. From Waterfalls by TLC to I Wanna Be Down by Brandy, each song had meaning then but even more meaning now.

"Hey," Ivory sighed as Roman lifted her arm over her head, twirling her on her wheels and then pulling her back in to the sanctity of his muscular form. They were connected, completely, and moved effortlessly in perfect harmony. It was perfection, and they were both having a good time. There were smiles and laughter and connection in more than a physical way, and they both felt it. The feeling was undeniable; no trepidation, no speculation, simply the ability to enjoy each other's company completely.

And then, the first bars of "Make It Last Forever," by Keith Sweat cruised through the surround sound speakers. It was a whole mood. It was one of the hottest songs from their past that still resonated to this day. Although it was Roman's playlist that entertained the duo, he still responded to the music as though it were a pleasant surprise. And when he spun Ivory into him, positioning her in front with him skating immediately behind her, their bodies connected again. It was a slow jam, and Ivory and Roman skated smoothly, with her head resting comfortably against the strength of his chest, and his chiseled arms wrapped tightly around the firm of her waist. His glide became her glide, their bodies inseparable. One slow jam became two and then a string of them that kept the duo closer than close. She felt so good in his arms, and Roman inhaled deeply. He wanted her essence to inhabit him fully. The rise of Ivory's round ass pressed against him and the undulation of her thick hips as they moved to the beat gave his nature a rise that he couldn't deny, and that Ivory instantly felt. She didn't run away from him, though. Those amorous feelings were something she quietly shared even though she continued to be surprised by how deeply she felt for Roman.

Undeniable...

That's what he felt.

She felt it too...

# Chapter Sixteen

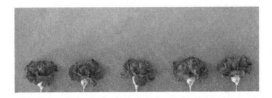

"*M*ake it last forever," Roman sang, leaning in against Ivory's ear.

The baritone of his voice strummed through her, striking her feminine chords and settling in the pit of her stomach.

Apprehension...

The way he held her, the way Roman made her feel, the apprehension that Ivory held on to slowly widdled away. She worked to silence the voice in her head; that cautionary voice that made Ivory question what she felt; what her head and heart couldn't seem to come to agreement on. The always practical Ivory didn't feel like being practical in the moment. Roman made her feel beautiful and sexy, and desirable, and for the first time, Ivory gave in to how he made her feel. Slowly, she lifted her arm and reached up, cradling Roman's head, pulling him even closer to her. He breathed against her ear again and then lightly kissed her lobe. Roman's sweet touch sent a wave of warm chills straight to Ivory's soul. She could barely contain the electrifying sensations that pulsed through her and Roman felt her quiver under his hold. But he wanted to see her face, to engage her totally. With one smooth move, Roman spun Ivory in his hands, turning her to face him as they still glided across the rink floor.

As she spun around, Ivory inhaled as she felt the strength of Roman's arms holding her close. She exhaled against his chest, and slowly, her arms traced upwards to find him gazing down at her. Ivory felt completely enraptured in the depths of the way Roman looked at her. He didn't need words to convey what he was feeling. Everything about the way he took her in with his dark, brooding eyes was enough. When Roman leaned in, eradicating the space between them, Ivory laced her arms around Roman's neck, not shrinking from his intensity. Their lips connected, softly, sweetly; yet, a firestorm of salacious pulsations inhabited both and the sweetness of the kiss quickly faded. There was a mutual hunger, a desire that couldn't be quenched. He thirsted for her and devoured her mouth as though she offered sweet succulence. Roman's tongue explored the softness of Ivory's mouth and she responded in kind, causing a catechism of hot passionate entanglement.

Ivory hummed against Roman's lips, and the vibrations that poured through him were more than he could handle. He couldn't get enough of her and lifted her from the floor, pulling Ivory as close as possible. She couldn't be too close. There was no such thing. Roman craved that connection, and his lips told her so. Ivory's jewel thumped hard as she felt the press of his manhood against her. Their entanglement reached a fevered pitch. It was getting harder and harder for either of them to contain themselves. Roman didn't want to pressure Ivory; there was too much at risk. However, his manly inclinations were difficult to suppress.

But he had to control himself. Ivory meant too much to Roman for him to bend to his flesh. As their lips parted, his eyes engaged her once again. Slowly, Roman lowered Ivory, so her skates touched the rink floor, but he felt her knees give way, and he held onto to her tightly. Ivory held on tight to him as well.

"You okay?" Roman asked.

A slight smile parted Ivory's full lips.

"You've got my knees weak," she hummed. Ivory's confession made her blush, and she buried her face against Roman's chest. He liked the way that sounded. He was weak for her, too. Without hesitation, Roman remedied the situation, once again lifting Ivory off her feet and cradling her in his arms.

"I wouldn't want you to fall," Roman crooned; his eyes narrow and hooded.

"Ah," she exclaimed as she felt herself being lifted. *This is so embarrassing*, Ivory thought to herself; yet, the smile on her face couldn't be denied. Roman was careful with her as they made their way back to the sitting area. He stepped smoothly from the slick of the rink floor to the carpet and didn't stop until he had placed Ivory comfortably on the bench. Roman sat down next to her, and the two fell quiet. The whirl of the spinning lights continued to light up their surroundings, and the sounds of rhythmic rhythm and blues filled the space.

"So many memories here, you know," Ivory mused.

"Good memories," Roman added.

"Thanks for this," Ivory said, turning slightly to bring Roman's face into her purview. "It was a surprise," Ivory playfully fussed, "but a good one."

"So, you'll forgive me for the surprise part?" Roman teased.

"This time," Ivory quipped.

There was an easy smile shared between them.

"Are you ready," Roman asked. Ivory nodded her head. It had been a good evening, but being back on skates after so many years had her legs feeling like spaghetti. Admittedly, Roman played a part in that. He eased from the bench and positioned himself in front of her to take her skates off. He didn't give Ivory a chance to do it herself, and she learned to be okay with his chivalry.

Although Roman had large hands, he was incredibly gentle with her. The rise of her skirt caught Roman's attention, exposing the deliciousness of her mocha thighs. Their previous kiss still tingled on his lips, and although he tried desperately to keep his primal nature under control, Ivory made it difficult, without effort. As Roman eased the thick socks from her legs, his hands caressed her flesh, and he placed her bare feet on his thighs so they wouldn't touch the carpeted floor. Ivory noticed just how much care he took with her, thinking about things other men wouldn't even consider. Roman was a perfect gentleman, and his hands on her naked flesh sent sensations surging up to her center. Resistance was futile, and Ivory knew that to be true. Reaching out, she wrapped her arms around Roman's neck and pulled him in close. She couldn't deny the way he made her feel and for the first time since their chance encounter, Ivory stopped thinking. Roman melded into her pull and knelt between her legs, lifting his frame to meet her lips.

Roman stopped just short of kissing her. His eyes fell to the shape of her full lips, and he felt her exhale against his face. The magnetism and intensity at that moment was palatable. The energy surge was high, and their auras danced and intertwined, creating a cocoon of scintillating pressure destined to explode. But Roman didn't kiss her. And for a split second, Ivory thought she might have made a mistake. Her mouth paused on a gasp as Roman eased away from her. She felt his warm hands move up her legs, from her calves to her thighs. And when he lowered his head and kissed where his hands had been, abandonment was no longer an issue for Ivory. Her hands had fallen casually to the bench. But as Romans tender lips moved from her knees to the inside of one thigh and then the other, Ivory's fingers gripped the bench as shots of heated energy scorched through her.

Ivory's puss thumped, but she couldn't squeeze her thighs together because Roman was there. And the kisses he trailed up her thighs, comingled with the vibrato of the hum that buzzed on his lips, caused fresh dew to spill from her jewel.

"Roman," she whispered, wanting him to stop but not wanting him to stop.

Ivory reached for Roman again, coaxing his head from her as he languished more hot kisses to her flesh.

"Roman," she whispered again, the angst on her lips reflecting the tightening in her core. Ivory was practically whimpering as her nipples hardened with anticipation. Roman loved the way she tasted and hungrily kissed every inch of her. Her mouth called his name, and Ivory's legs gave way, falling open for more of what drove her insane. Roman's lips trailed higher, closer to her feminine essence. He could smell her titillating scent, and his mouth watered in response. He had to have her. There was no going back. And Ivory didn't want him to, not at this point. She cradled the back of Roman's head as he made his way to her crown.

With his fingers, Roman eased her silken panties to the side and tasted Ivory's essence for the first time. His dick was hard and throbbed, pressing against the confines of his clothing. Roman had to have more, and he licked her jewel, savoring the taste of her. He sucked softly at her crown's lips and moaned against her. The guttural sounds that passed through Roman's lips comingled with the sounds of exquisite passion that passed through Ivory's as her head dropped between her shoulders. As Roman's mouth sent waves of pleasure dancing through her, Ivory could hardly be still. Her hands moved from the back of his head to gripping the edge of the bench again. Her hips lifted as his mouth tantalized and teased her; his tongue finding her clit and assuaging it with long, slow licks.

"Shit," Ivory gasped as her body convulsed from her first orgasm, coating Roman's tongue with sweet honeydew. Roman couldn't be inhibited and paused from drinking her in, only long enough to rip her panties, moving them out of the way. He reengaged, and hummed inside her, swallowing every drop of her essence. Ivory needed relief. She couldn't take her body's cravings for him. Easing her head from her shoulders and lifting her hands from the bench, Ivory placed her hands on Roman's broad shoulders.

"Please, Roman," she moaned.

Reluctantly, he lifted his head, and his eyes found hers. She could see her moisture on his lips, and as he licked them, Ivory leaned forward, kissing his lips ravishingly and tasting herself there. Her hands fell to his waist, and without words, told Roman what she wanted – what she needed as her hands trailed to his belt buckle. His hands fell on top of hers and they connected, their eyes searching the eyes of the other. Both trepidatious and wary of what this could mean but both desperately wanting to experience the other in the most intimate way. Ivory's eyes closed slowly, and the mink of her lashes fluttered against her brown skin. She opened them and looked into Roman's eyes.

He had the confirmation he needed, and they both moved to release what she desired most. Time moved fast and stood perfectly still at the same time. Ivory needed him inside her. That was the only way her body would be relieved. Roman needed to be inside her. That was the only way his body would be relieved. Roman unbuckled his belt and unbuttoned his slacks. Ivory's eyes fell to the rise in his briefs. His manliness was pronounced, and Ivory's eyes widened a little. Still, she craved him. Leaning in, Ivory kissed him again while simultaneously tracing the edge of his briefs, sliding them off Roman's hips. He reached for her, wrapping his arms around her waist. Ivory eased to the edge of the bench, as her legs quivered in anticipation.

Roman moved forward as his dick throbbed wantonly.

"I want to see you," he crooned, lifting his hand to her chin and inclining Ivory's head until their eyes met. With his other hand, Roman guided himself to the tip of her folds. His heart pounded like a locomotive in his chest. This moment... this was the one he dreamed of, fantasized about, desired for as long as Roman could remember. Ivory's soft eyes invited him in, and they remained locked in a fervid gaze as Roman's manhood found the fullness of her jewel.

"Ahhhh," she gasped, feeling the fullness of him gradually, slowly ease inside her. The walls of Ivory's puss softened and gave way to his thickness, and Roman maintained her eyes as he felt her folds welcoming him in.

"Bae," he uttered. Even that small utterance was choked in Roman's throat. Ivory's gentle hand found the side of his handsomely rugged face and caressed him there as they remained locked in a heart-pounding gaze. Ivory felt his thickness pulsing inside her. Looking into the truth of Roman's eyes, she finally understood what his lips told her; that he had always loved her. There was a dull ache in her pounding heart that was quickly overcome as Roman pushed deeper inside her.

"Nnhnn," Ivory moaned as the tip of his manhood hit her clit. Her body convulsed again, and it was her primal instinct that took over. Lifting from the bench, Ivory wrapped her arms around Roman's thickly corded neck, trusting his strength to balance her as she eased down on top of him, giving of herself fully to him.

"Uhhh," he exhaled as he felt her folds give way to him, and her thighs pressed against his. Wrapping his arms around her back, Roman pulled Ivory close, and they fell into a slow rhythm, her pressing down on his thickness and him thrusting up inside her jewel. Her head fell to the crease of his neck as she allowed herself to be lost in the moment. Ivory hadn't been touched, not like this, ever and every part of her body said so. Roman felt her hard nipples brushing against his chest as their bodies melded into one.

They became one flesh...

There was an urgency inside Ivory, and she gyrated faster on top of him. The strength of Roman's legs held her as he met every push with a push of his own.

"I can't," she started, the words stopping short in her throat. She was on the verge of another climax, and Ivory couldn't control it.

"Ivory," he whispered against her ear. She was fucking him with reckless abandon. But it was more than that. This was a soul connection, and Roman felt it as his own sense of urgency roared inside him. The thickness of his dick swelled even more as the hotness of her puss enveloped him. He couldn't hold on much longer, but he never wanted to let her go.

Her pant against his neck nearly sent Roman into orbit. He felt Ivory's body shivering against him.

"I can't, I can't," she whimpered, lifting her head from his shoulder and shaking it back and forth as her body was racked with jolting spasm after spasm. Roman felt thick wetness coating his dick, as cum poured from her.

"Rrrrrggggghhhhh."

He squeezed her tight as hot gism pushed from the depths of his manhood into the warm folds of Ivory's crown. He filled Ivory to capacity as their love juices poured one from the other. But her body didn't stop. Ivory's head fell forward, and she found the fold of his neck again, burying her head there as another wave of orgasm coursed through her.

# Chapter Seventeen

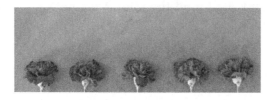

ONE WEEK LATER

*T*he sisters were glad to be together one more time. It wasn't often that all their schedules aligned so that they could make something like this possible; however, the Moore girls knew how important family was, and they did what it took to make sure they got together as often as possible. Although most times, the sisters went out for mani/pedis, shopping, or dining, this time they were at home, Kennedy's home so she could be included in the festivities.

"Samantha, you are the best," Trinity exclaimed as the four masseuses lined up their chairs to cater to the women's needs.

"I just thought this would be something different," Samantha replied, "something we could enjoy together in the comfort of Kennedy's home, so she didn't have to go too far."

Trekking down to her family room was a lot easier than venturing out of the house. Even though physically, she had pretty much recovered from her son's birth, Kennedy wasn't ready to be too far away from him.

"Yes, Sam, this is wonderful," Kennedy sighed as the masseuse provided her with a deep tissue massage. "Chile, I just hope he don't make my milk come down with all this good rubbing."

The sisters fell out laughing. Kennedy still had her crazy sense of humor, and the girls loved it.

"And it doesn't hurt that these brothers are fine as hell," Trinity mumbled, only loud enough for her sisters to hear. Or so she thought. But when one of the male technicians lifted his head and winked at Trinity, she flushed. He heard her.

Of course, the Moore sisters kept it classy. There were two men, masseuses, and two women, all licensed, all professional. While four sisters were in the chairs, the other sisters enjoyed mimosas and good food, all prepared by Bryce. He had help in the kitchen from some of the men folk – Evan, Kingston, Lance, and Nicholas. Although they couldn't cook as well as Bryce, they were there for moral support and taste testing.

In the midst of laughs and conversation, a phone chimed.

"If that's mine," Emery moaned, relaxing in her shoulders, "let it go to voicemail. I don't want any interruptions right now." Her comment made the technician smile.

The phone chimed again.

"It's mine," Ivory commented, sitting her glass down and picking up her phone.

"Uhn," Daphne uttered, teasing Ivory by looking over her shoulder, trying to see who was calling. Ivory saw her sister sneaking a peek and stepped to the side, shielding her phone before swiping it.

"You play too much," Ivory giggled.

"What you hiding it for then?" Daphne teased again.

Ivory laughed as she turned her back to her sisters and read the text message.

*Hey, beautiful. I pray this message finds you well. I'm supposed to be working, but I can't concentrate. I can't stop thinking about you. I miss you desperately, Ivory. I hope to be back in the states in about a week. I need to see you. Can you make some time for me?*

Ivory felt warmness rising from her center to the heights of her cheekbones. Yet, she didn't know how to respond to his request. Once again, Ivory felt herself torn between the past and present and what that could mean for her future. She blew a heavy sigh between her pursed lips. She didn't want to leave Roman hanging, but at the same time, Ivory didn't want to say the wrong thing. Instead of answering, Ivory swiped the phone, shutting it down, picking up her glass once again. With one gulp, she downed the libation remaining in her glass and quickly refilled it to the brim. There was no pause in Ivory quickly drinking that one down either.

"Uhm, you okay?" Aubrey asked, noticing her sister's antics. Ivory had never been a big drinker, and although it was mimosa, there was enough liquor in it to get you buzzed.

Ivory had the glass fully tilted in the air, drinking the mimosa to the last drop. She could feel the cool concoction warming her belly as the alcohol hit her system. As she sat the glass down on the table, she offered Aubrey a wayward smile.

"Yep, I'm fine."

"The hell you say," Samantha chimed in. She noticed Ivory's uncharacteristic behavior, too.

"I said I'm fine," Ivory sighed. But her tone didn't match the strength of her words. She wasn't fine, and everyone in the room could tell.

"Ivory," Felicity said, moving into her sister's space and gaining her attention. "Stop saying that, okay? You are so not fine right now."

"And if you don't want to talk about it, that's cool," Daphne added, "but please stop lying to yourself and us."

Ivory heard what her sisters had to say. They were right. She wasn't fine. But that's what was easiest to say, especially when you're supposed to be strong – a strong Black woman at that. Saying 'I'm fine' is what people really want to hear. They don't want to hear about your problems or your pains. But Ivory had to remember, this was her family. They weren't just people. These were her sisters, and they for damn sure wasn't falling for the bullshit.

"I bet it's that man," Trinity quipped with her face tucked into the comfort of the massage chair and of the male masseuses – the one who winked, going to work on her back. Trinity made it her business to get in his chair when it became available, and it was a move she didn't regret.

"What man?" Kennedy and Aubrey asked in unison.

"Ro – man!" Trinity squealed, lifting her face from the chair and doing a little shimmy shake for emphasis. The male masseuse didn't miss the wiggle in her ass as he stepped back to watch her move.

Ivory's eyes rolled to the top of her head. *She can't keep shit,* Ivory thought, feeling all of her sister's eyes on her. The only person unfamiliar with Roman was Samantha, but that unfamiliarity wouldn't last long.

"Roman? Roman?" Emery repeated.

"You mean, Little Roman from back in the day, Roman?" Felicity asked.

All Ivory could do was narrow her eyes and shoot Trinity the death stare.

The sisters who knew him were eyeballing Ivory, waiting on a response. She couldn't bring herself to respond, but once again, Trinity was there to provide all the answers. She lifted a delicate finger to her technician, asking him to pause as she offered some insight.

"Yes, honey, that Roman. But he ain't Lil' Roman no more, is he Ivory?"

She didn't wait for Ivory to answer. Trinity saw the confused look on Samantha's face and went on, despite her sister's obvious embarrassment.

"Roman was Ivory's bestie back in the day. She ran into him at the embassy, and there have been fireworks ever since."

"So not surprised," Aubrey offered.

"Me either," Kennedy added.

Ivory looked from one sister to the other through

narrowed eyes. Her brow was furrowed, and her mouth was slightly ajar.

"Why are you looking like that?" Emery chimed. "Anyone with eyes could tell that boy was crazy about you."

"And baby, that ain't changed a bit," Trinity chimed.

If she could have folded in herself from all the visual pressure she felt, Ivory would have done just that. She knew the information Trinity provided didn't give the answers her sisters wanted, nor did it explain why she was acting the way she did.

"Well," Charity said as she folded her arms across her flat belly.

Charity was the last holdout of the sisters applying pressure. With her joining in, Ivory knew she had some explaining to do.

"What?" She defended. Ivory had no intention of giving in so quickly to the undo pressure.

"Why are you drinkin' like you drinkin', since you want to go about this the long way," Charity pressed.

"Because," Ivory huffed, sounding like she did when she was much younger. The girls weren't going for it, though, and were willing to wait for her explanation. There was some hesitation on the part of Ivory, but that hesitation didn't last long.

"He told me he loved me."

An eerie quiet fell over the room, and Ivory found herself looking from one sister to the other, awaiting what she knew would be a snarky reply.

Finally, Daphne spoke. "And you're surprised by that?"

Ivory expected snark, but Daphne's inquiry wasn't that at all. Ivory felt that it was genuine, which was somewhat disarming. Ivory plunked down in the chair that was closest to her, exhaling an even heavier sigh than before. Although her head was starting to spin, she reached for her glass. Finding it empty, Ivory reached for the mimosa but was quickly intercepted by Samantha standing nearby. Ivory looked up at her big sister, questioning the intervention. Samantha shook her head and moved the carafe of drink out of Ivory's reach.

"Answer the question, Ivory, are you surprised?" Daphne repeated.

"Yes," she finally admitted.

"Girl," Trinity huffed.

"No, Trinity," Kennedy stepped in. "Don't," Ken continued. "If she genuinely didn't know, she didn't know."

"But how, though?" Trinity insisted. "It was so damn obvious."

"To you," Ivory clapped back. "It was obvious to you. Still, no matter what you saw then, this is different."

"It is," Charity agreed. "Because this time, this ain't no puppy love."

"Right," Ivory acquiesced.

"So, what's the problem," Sam asked, piecing enough of the story together during the conversation.

"Cause," Ivory sighed. "I knew him one way. I loved him that way, but as a friend." Ivory paused as she tried to work out the quandary in her own head. The technicians were done, having rendered their services well. Quietly, they packed their equipment, but not before the masseuse that worked on Trinity slid her his phone number. The deep conversation between the sisters was halted while they made their exit but quickly resumed. The sisters weren't going to let it go and awaited Ivory's explanation.

"You were saying, Ivory?" Felicity questioned.

"Now, I feel like I don't even know him, not for real, not as the person he was to me."

"Is that necessarily a bad thing, though?" Aubrey asked.

"Ya'll don't understand," Ivory quickly combatted.

"Then explain it, Ivory," Emery suggested. "You know we are here to listen no matter what and help if you want it."

"It's just so much all at once," Ivory began, receiving what Emery had to say and trusting her sisters in the process. "First, he told me that the whole time I knew him, we knew him back in the day, his family was wealthy. Can you believe that? And I don't mean a little rich, but like billionaire level rich."

There were some surprised looks on a few of her sister's faces.

"And then to tell me that he has always loved me? Like when we were kids, he felt that way about me? I feel like I was deceived like he was a stranger. I felt like it undermined our whole relationship."

Ivory paused as she mused aloud, no longer just responding to her sister's inquiry but working out her thoughts for herself.

"If he was dishonest with me all this time, how can I trust what he's saying today?"

"I feel that," Charity sighed. She'd been through a similar situation with her own man, O'Shea. They had been friends, the best of friends, and became lovers. So, if no one else got it, the second guessing, the questioning, the mental torment of trying to make the right decision, Charity certainly did.

"But do you love him?"

The question was piercing and stung Ivory's troubled heart. She knew what her mind told her. She knew what her heart felt. She knew how he made her feel. Those things were not on one accord, not in her conscious mind. Ivory looked around the room, trying to read her sister's faces. She had been so deep in her own thoughts; she wasn't sure which one raised the question. And then the question was raised again.

"Ivory, do you love him?"

It was Kennedy who had spoken. Instantly, Ivory felt some kind of way because of the relationship she had with Ken and the experiences Kennedy recently had, solidifying her love with the birth of her son.

"I don't know if I should," Ivory replied. "Roman told me that he loves me."

"And what did you say?" Kennedy continued.

"I know."

The typical response when a person says they love you is to return the sentiment in kind. Yet, Ivory hadn't done that. Understanding brought a wave of unanticipated emotion, and Ivory found herself nearly on the brink of tears. How could she have been blind for so long? How could she have missed that, and what the hell was she supposed to do with it? Every girl longs for that one man who would love her without condition... that would put her first, make her his priority. That was not a question in Ivory's mind. She knew, she understood that Roman loved her. Yet, she battled with how to feel about it. It became more and more difficult to quell the rise of emotion that swirled in her belly. Her sisters saw how hard their sister fighting to hold back the tears.

"Aw, babe," Daphne consoled, sitting down in the seat next to Ivory and wrapping her arm around her back.

Although Trinity had been quick to respond before, feeling like Ivory should have known certain things, she hesitated to say anything more. She saw how her sister was struggling. Trinity didn't want to add insult to injury. She didn't want to be hurtful, understanding that Ivory was in flux. What seemed so obvious to Trinity wasn't so clear to Ivory, and hearing her sister's responses drove that home for the youngest Moore girl.

"I just don't know what to do," Ivory hummed. A single tear teetered on her lids, and she recklessly swiped it with the back of her hand, refusing to allow the saltiness to trickle onto her face.

Neither of her sisters was quick to respond. Her emotionality made sense to them, and none of them wanted to discount how she felt with a snippy response. In their own way, they all could relate to that moment when they questioned what the disagreement between what the heart said and what the mind said.

"Do you want to love him?" Emery asked.

The room fell quiet, and Emery noticed Ivory's lip quivering, a tell-tale sign that it was becoming more difficult to hold back the tears.

"It's okay to cry if you need to, sis," Felicity sighed. "We've all done it at one time or another."

"Cause relationship shit ain't easy," Trinity huffed. Although she wasn't currently in a relationship, that didn't mean Trinity couldn't relate. She'd had her heart broken a time or two, much like her sisters.

"No, it is not," Daphne concurred. "So, do what yo need to do. If you need to cry, baby girl, then let them tears fall."

"I know that's right," Aubrey agreed.

Many of the Moore girls were happy in their current relationships, but it didn't take but a short trip down memory lane to remind them how painful this kind of situation could be and was. It was Charity who was the one to respond. Slowly, she walked over to her sister and knelt down in front of her, taking Ivory's hands into her own. Charity waited until Ivory was ready to engage her before speaking. But it took Ivory a moment. Just the gentle touch of her sister's hands caused the tears to spill onto her cheeks. This time, Ivory wasn't in the position to swipe them away. They fell, and she had to accept it because the tears needed to happen. Ivory needed to have that moment, where her feelings spilled over, manifesting themselves in the form of hot tears on her warmed cheeks.

"Whatever you're feeling, however you're feeling, Ivory, it's right for you," Charity began. "Nobody can tell you how to feel, because your feelings belong solely to you. The real question is, whether you are willing to take a risk with your heart? And I know, like you do, people say life is a risk, and they're right. But only you can decide, is Roman worth the risk?"

Charity's words were like an accelerant, and tears flowed freely from Ivory's eyes. She heard her sister with her ears and listened with her heart. Ivory didn't need to respond. Charity wasn't looking for one. She just hoped that her sister would consider what she said when making her decision.

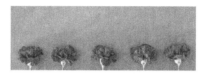

# Chapter Eighteen

*R*oman checked his phone again. Still, there had been no response from Ivory. He didn't want to seem desperate and ask again. He didn't want to pressure her and possibly risk Ivory declining his request to see her when he returned to the States. Roman held the phone, staring at it.

"Bro, what's up with you?"

The question came from longtime friend and business associate, Michael Chamberlain.

"Huh?"

Even then, Roman was distracted. Fortunately, the boardroom had emptied of the investors Roman met with. He had been able to focus enough to conduct business successfully, but a friend like Michael could see through the business façade to see that there was something pressing on Roman's mind. Roman turned the phone face down on the table, but his ears stayed pricked, hoping to hear it buzz.

Michael sat down across from Roman.

"I said, what's on your mind? Obviously, it's something important."

Roman shook his head. "Not a what, man."

"Oh," Michael uttered, sitting forward in his seat and resting his elbows on the table. "Who is she?"

"Why are you assuming it's a woman?" Roman chuffed.

"Because, there is not one man on this earth, other than your father, who could distract you like this. And the last time we spoke, you and pops were on good terms. Has that changed?" Michael challenged.

"Naw," Roman chortled. "Me and dad still good."

"Then, who is she?" Michael reiterated.

Roman blew out a long slow breath of air through his lips. He was so busted, and he knew it. He leaned back in the leather, executive chair he was sitting in.

"Ivory Moore."

"Oh," Michael replied. That was a name he hadn't heard in a while. A knowing smile eased across his lips, and he steepled his hands in front of him. "So, I take it that last trip to Atlanta was interesting, huh?"

Michael knew Roman visited the Sudanese Embassy during his last excursion in the south, but since the visit, Roman hadn't said much about it. Maybe Ivory was the reason why.

"Interesting," Roman repeated. "You could say that." Roman's words didn't reveal much, but Michael knew him well enough to read between the lines.

"So, what are you going to do about her?" Michael asked. "She's always been the one."

"Why do you say that?"

"Because, man, there have been all kinds of women interested in you. Some you've entertained, most you haven't. But you never talk about them. They never distracted you, never. You've always been able to keep whatever relationship you had in check without it interfering in business. But during this meeting, you weren't there, not like usual."

"I was on point," Roman defended, but not strongly.

"True, you were," Michael agreed, "after someone called your name and waited for you to get your head out of the clouds and respond," Michael chuckled.

"That bad, huh?"

"For real," Michael affirmed.

"Damn."

Hearing Michael's comments put things into perspective for Roman. Not that he needed someone else to tell him that Ivory was on his mind. He couldn't stop thinking about her. He just hadn't realized how much thinking about her spilled over into his business. Yet, Roman knew he couldn't stop thinking about her. He didn't want to. He just had to be more vigilant when it came to keeping his fixation on her in check. And maybe he would be able to if he felt like they were on solid ground. However, as hard as it might be to accept, Roman understood why they weren't... not yet.

"All Im'ma say is, if she means that much to you, do something about it."

And with that, Michael stood up from the chair and left the room.

Roman watched him go. He wasn't compelled to leave just yet. The room was empty, quiet, a place where he could think, undisturbed, and contemplate. And his thoughts were of Ivory. Methodically, Roman's eyes trailed across the empty room and then landed on his phone. It hadn't buzzed. He picked it up, checking to make sure he didn't have the phone on silent. If Ivory had responded, Roman didn't want to miss it. But there was nothing. No text. No missed call. Maybe she didn't want to see him again?

BOTH IVORY AND ROMAN HAD A SLEEPLESS NIGHT. BOTH WERE encumbered by the words of people they trusted combined with their own tortured thoughts. But the things that prevented them from peaceful slumber were different, yet intriguingly connected. Roman was glad that the secrets he revealed to Ivory hadn't completely turned her off from him. There was no doubt in Roman's mind that Ivory was the only woman for him, and his mind traveled back to that night at the skating rink; how she looked, how she smelled, the way Ivory felt in his arms and the way her body showed him what words were unable to say. Yet, the fact that she didn't reciprocate his 'I love you' did sting a little. Roman understood why she didn't say it, though. He understood with his intellectual mind, but a man's heart is different. His level of pride is different – not right or wrong, just different. Roman didn't want his masculine pride to begrudge Ivory the time she needed to feel what she needed to feel. He didn't want Ivory to respond out of obligation, compulsory and less than heartfelt. Roman wanted her to love him genuinely and for her words to be a reflection of what she truly felt in her heart. So, he knew he had to be patient with her and not rush Ivory to a place where he'd been for a long time. More than anything, Roman didn't want to do anything to frighten her away. He couldn't risk losing Ivory forever. His heart couldn't take that.

*Patience*, Roman repeated as he tried desperately to drift off to sleep. *Patience…*

She'd tossed and turned for several nights in a row, not just tonight. After her date with Roman, Ivory found it hard to sleep. She felt like, in some ways, her body defied her even though her body couldn't act without her permission. Maybe it was guilt she felt. She'd never been the kind of girl for a one-night stand or screwing on the first date. That was not her modus operandi. Yet, she did with Roman, and although her body had been completely satiated by the intensity of his touch, she wasn't forced or gave of herself reluctantly, Ivory felt like she should feel guilty. But that wasn't a genuine feeling, not for her, not this time. Although this was her first date with Roman, he wasn't someone new, not totally. But did she love him? That question is what caused the endless restlessness. Should she love him? Was this thing moving too fast?

Ivory felt like her heart was racing ahead of her, responding and reacting in ways she couldn't control. She was slow to love, always had been. She never gave of herself too easily for fear of being hurt. Ivory had seen too much of what loving the wrong man could do, and she didn't want that kind of grief for herself. Clearly, though, she wasn't in complete control this time, because her heart, her emotions, her feelings were miles ahead of her, and Ivory struggled to catch up. Which part of her was right? The slow, practical part or the throw caution to the wind and live part?

There were so many examples of real love, admirable love around her. Could that kind of pure, unadulterated love be available to her?

Ivory didn't know. Maybe, just maybe, she was afraid to find out.

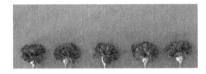

THE MID-MORNING SUN FOUND ITS WAY INTO IVORY'S BEDROOM through the smallest gap in her drapes. Although narrow, the brightness of the light was enough to break the darkness. Apparently, sleep found Ivory, and she wanted it to continue. But as the sun settled high in the sky, the trail of light landed on Ivory's face. Still, she refused to open her eyes and groaned as she turned over, covering her head with a feather pillow.

"Uhn," she mumbled, trying to settle back down and hold on to the last vestiges of slumber. But once her hard won sleep had been disturbed, Ivory found it hard to settle back in. Frustrated, she rolled over, tossing the pillow to the side and sitting up in the bed. As she did most times after waking, Ivory stretched and then reached for her cell phone.

Her eyes were still cloudy, and her blinks were slow as she swiped the screen to see the time. And then she remembered the message from the day before; the message she still hadn't answered.

*Dammit!*

Shaking her head, Ivory pulled up the message from Roman read it again. *Can you make some time for me?*

She released the phone, allowing it to fall into her lap, and then flopped back down on the bed. Ivory still didn't know what to say. Did she want to see him? That would be nice. She always had a good time with Roman, and the last time they were together was no different. Except, he professed his love to her. They experienced each other in a completely different way. They connected on a level that exceeded anything she could have ever imagined.

But those things she wouldn't say. Still, Roman deserved a response. After contemplating a few more minutes, Ivory lifted the phone from her lap.

*I apologize for not responding sooner.*

*Yes, I can make some time for you. Nothing fancy. No surprises.*

*Agreed?*

After hitting send, Ivory placed the phone on the side of the bed. If Roman didn't immediately respond, that would be okay. It'd taken her the whole night to comment. Instead of waiting by the phone, Ivory decided to take the trek to the restroom. She felt sluggish, so it took her a minute to sit up, swing her feet over the side of the bed, stand, and then walk across the floor. She didn't bother to turn on the light. There was enough of that peeping through the window in her bathroom to illuminate the space. Ivory ran her fingers through her curly afro, pushing the locs away from her face. With her eyes half-closed, she reached for her toothbrush and paste. After loading the brush, she methodically cleaned her teeth and then ran water to rinse her mouth. Although refreshing, it wasn't enough to wake her up, though, and Ivory wasn't sure she wanted to be fully awake, not yet, especially since she didn't have any major obligations for the day. She made her way back to her bed and slid in under the warm covers.

Even when Ivory wasn't trying to think about Roman, inevitably, thoughts of him invaded her mind. She didn't want to be in flux about him. She was sure most would not. Why would they? Roman was incredibly handsome, intelligent, sexy, funny, and kind. Those were admirable qualities Ivory experienced firsthand. She had to chuckle, though, because if anyone had asked what she looked for in a man, she would answer with attributes that described Roman. There was so much of him that was absolutely right, perfectly ideal. But were there more secrets yet to be revealed? Were there other things she didn't know about him? That's the part that unnerved Ivory as much as the overpowering, cataclysmic rollercoaster of emotions she felt when he was around.

When the phone rang, Ivory was plucked from her own internal dialog.

Lifting herself onto her elbow, Ivory picked up the

phone. Seeing his name populate the screen, Ivory's heart skipped a beat in her chest. She expected a text message, not a phone call. The phone rang again. On the other end, Roman wondered if she would answer. He was glad when she finally answered and affirmatively at that. But there was something about the tone of her response that made him want to call instead of responding in kind. Now, he just hoped she would pick up the phone. Roman paced the floor of his hotel room, waiting for Ivory to respond.

*Shit!* It would have been much easier if he just texted. Ivory sat up fully in her bed and exhaled slowly. Why was she tripping so hard about a phone call? This had never happened to her before, not when it came to Roman. Her nervousness was an indication that there had been a cosmic shift in their relationship.

*Okay*, Ivory said to herself. *Be cool.* She didn't know whether to sound cheerful or nonchalant, how to greet him or what he would say, but she swiped the phone and placed it to her ear.

"Hello."

Roman heard the formality of her salutation.

"Hello, Ivory," he replied in kind. "Am I disturbing you?"

"No, no," she answered, still trying to find her feet. "How are you? Where are you?"

The more she got Roman to talk, the more of an opportunity Ivory had to figure out how she would handle the conversation.

"I'm good," Roman answered. "Better now that I hear your voice."

"That's sweet of you to say," Ivory answered.

Something was off. Roman could feel it, and he didn't like it.

"Are you sure you're okay?"

"Yeah," Ivory said, trying to sound lighthearted. "I'm good."

Her words didn't reflect her tone. Roman knew what he had to do. Instead of pacing, he walked to his closet, balancing the phone on his neck, and slid his suits into their case, and then strode to the bathroom and packed his essentials. Within minutes, Roman was headed towards the door.

"I don't believe you."

Roman made his way to the elevator from his penthouse suite. He impatiently waited for the doors to open, and when they did, Roman hit the button quickly and repeatedly trying to compel the elevator to move faster.

"Why would you say that?" Ivory defended, caught off guard by his accuracy and responsiveness.

"Because I know you," Roman countered. "Remember, I know you."

She knew that to be true and had no response. There was silence between the two of them, and for the first time, the silence was awkward and uncomfortable.

"We need to talk, but not like this," Roman suggested.

"I thought we were talking," Ivory replied, trying to sound as regular as possible.

"No, not really," Roman insisted. "Not like we usually do."

His assessment was right, and she had no counter or quick-witted comeback. Ivory could hear a lot of movement in the background. At times the phone sounded muffled, and then it was clear. She deflected the conversation.

"What's going on wherever you are?"

"I'm making my way to you." Roman heard her question, but it was irrelevant. Something was wrong. His heart and soul told him so.

"Huh? What do you mean?"

"Ivory, you mean too much to me for us to have this kind of conversation. I need to see you face to face," Roman explained. "So, I am on my way to see you."

"Wait! Roman, seriously?"

"I have never been more serious about anything in my life," Roman affirmed. "I'll see you soon."

He didn't wait for any further descending conversation from Ivory. He didn't wait for her to agree or disagree. Roman's mind was made up. He was on his way.

"What the entire hell?" Ivory mused aloud. She shook her head and collapsed down onto the bed. Ivory knew Roman was not kidding. She knew if he said he was on his way, he was on his way. All she could do was be prepared when he got there. But how could Ivory prepare herself for what could be the most important conversation of her life? How could she express to Roman what she wasn't clear about herself – the cadre of emotions that tore through her and soothed her at the same time. How could she articulate how much she loved him and how afraid she was to truly love him?

Yet, there was a part of Ivory that was amused by Roman's impromptu actions. That said, something about the kind of man he was and what she meant to him. The real question was whether she could be even more important to him than she'd always been and be okay with it. But there would be no sleep for Roman. His mind was racing. Although his quandary was different, he still felt mental anguish as he reread the cryptic text message Ivory sent. Roman knew Ivory. He knew her well. What she didn't say is what bothered him the most. Had he moved too fast, giving in to his primal desires? Had he spoken too soon, revealing too much about himself before they truly had an opportunity to reconnect?

# Chapter Nineteen

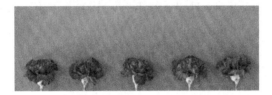

*R*oman didn't care about anything other than getting to Ivory. He contacted his pilot from the hotel lobby and told him to get the private jet ready. They were leaving early. Once on board, Roman had one message for the pilot.

"I don't care if you have to take this bitch to Mach 10, get me to Atlanta quickly and safely."

The pilot tipped his cap, acknowledging his instructions. Roman settled into the leather executive chair in his plane's office space. He took out his computer, thinking he could keep his mind occupied by doing some work. That worked for him in the past, so Roman thought he would give it a try. The engine of the jet roared underneath him and the seat-belt light came on. Roman paused, just long enough to buckle up and then tried to focus on work. He handled a few business calls and did some work online but Roman struggled. Soon, he found himself staring out of the window, lost in his own thoughts as the jet scathed through billowy clouds and the bluest sky.

Ivory didn't have any idea what time Roman would arrive. One thing she was certain of, however, he was on his way. At first, Ivory tried to blow it off like it was no big deal. She went about her day as though it was a normal day at home – some light housekeeping, doing the laundry, and prepping meals for the week with the cool sounds of all her favorite R&B hits playing in the background. Ivory danced through her house, doing what she ordinarily did on the weekend. But there was nothing normal about the situation, and before long, Ivory found herself inundated with thoughts of Roman; some good, some bad, but all riveting. But being stuck in mental flux was exhausting. She didn't want to think anymore, not about that. Ivory felt like her every waking thought revolved around her feelings – those she acknowledged and those she desperately tried to dismiss. Although Ivory had cleaned the guest bathroom, she found herself back in the small but beautifully decorated space. In her hand, she had her cleaning caddy with everything necessary to make the area spotless. Ivory started by cleaning all the glass surfaces and thinking of Roman. Before long, though, Ivory was on her hands and knees with a small brush, meticulously scrubbing the porcelain tiles and thinking of Roman.

The circles Ivory cleaned became smaller and smaller as her mind drifted back to that night at the skating rink. So much about that night was perfect. Whenever Ivory skated, she felt carefree and light. She felt that way on their date. She and Roman laughed and were able to be carefree and light together. They moved in perfect sync, harmoniously, as though they were one entity. And that feeling of singularity didn't end, only heightened when they crossed the threshold from friends to lovers. How could something that felt so right, feel so wrong afterwards?

"Because you think too damn much," Ivory scolded herself.

Her frustration spilled over. Ivory's mental exhaustion spilled over. She finished the mindless cleaning in the bathroom and made a decision. The only way to shut off her thoughts was to go back to bed. That's what she did. After a steaming hot shower and putting on fresh pajamas, Ivory darkened her room and climbed back into bed, hoping that her mind would be an absolute blank canvas so she could sleep peacefully.

Roman was going stir crazy. Although his private jet was spacious and luxurious, he felt like the curved walls were closing in on him. Unbuckling his seatbelt, Roman stood to his full height, the top of his head just inches from the crown of the plane. He couldn't sit still any longer. His mind was racing. Roman stepped out into the narrow aisle, making full use of the space. His long stride took him to the front of the jet, where he pivoted, paced to the back, and then again. He contemplated what he would say, but none of the words that came to him felt quite right. Their next encounter could either make or break their relationship before it even became solidified as the kind of relationship Roman desired.

But he didn't want to be desirous alone. The lone stewardess that manned the flight watched Mr. West pacing measuredly through the jet. She didn't disturb him, but she could tell something was bothering him. Whatever it was, the stewardess hoped he worked it out. She'd been his stewardess for a number of years and had observed many highs and some lows when it came to Mr. West. Whatever this was bothered him greatly. It was written all over his face.

Just then, there was a ding that rang through the jet's chamber, notifying of the need for seatbelts. Shortly after, the pilot came through.

"We will begin our descent into Atlanta in fifteen minutes. There may be some turbulence as it's raining in the Metro area."

Roman abbreviated his steps and returned to his executive chair, buckling up for the landing.

"Excuse me, Mr. West," the stewardess cut in, feeling like it was safe to do so. "Would you like me to have your car waiting on the tarmac?"

"Thanks, Crystal. Call my driver."

"Absolutely, Mr. West."

Before Crystal could turn to walk away, Roman's attention was already diverted out of the window. Darkness began to give way to light as he watched the city come into view. His vision was obscured as rain pelted the windows, blurring the lights below. Yet, Roman stayed focused on his destination as the jet descended.

The pilot maneuvered, keeping the aircraft as level as possible. A roar of thunder loudly assaulted their senses as the wheels of the jet touched down and then abruptly bumped and bumped again, causing the aircraft to waiver off its course. The pilot had to pull up sharply to try and reposition the jet for a smoother landing. Although Crystal was a seasoned stewardess, a slight gasp escaped her lips, and she gripped the arms of the chair she sat in. Roman's response wasn't as visceral, but his heart did pound in his chest behind the scare. All he wanted was the chance to see Ivory. He hoped that wasn't too much to ask of the Creator.

The pilot circled around, working to bring the private runway back into view. Roman could tell from the splatters on the window that it was raining even harder. Then, out of nowhere, there was another loud rumbling as thunder shook the atmosphere, quickly followed by blinding bright light as lightning cracked through the darkness. At first, Roman thought it wouldn't be a problem getting the jet to the tarmac. However, with the explosion of bad weather, now, he wasn't so sure. Although the seatbelt light was on, Roman couldn't be bothered with formalities. Within seconds, he was out of his seat and moving quickly towards the pilot's cabin.

"What's the plan?" Roman asked as he opened the door to the cockpit.

"Uh," the pilot began, keeping his eyes on the landscape in front of him. "I hope to be able to take another run at it and bring her down safely," the pilot explained. "But lightning is a problem."

Roman could see how focused the pilot was, and he appreciated that. But there was something he had to say.

"Listen, do what you have to do to land this plane safely," Roman insisted, "as soon as possible."

He didn't need to explain why it was important. His tone said it all.

"Yes sir, Mr. West," the pilot answered, acknowledging his bosses' request.

Roman disappeared as quickly as he had appeared and resumed his seat. He couldn't bear the thought of something happening to prevent him from seeing Ivory. Roman would see her tonight, if he had to will it so.

The harsh weather continued to crack and pound around them. It was as dangerous for the jet to remain in the air below the clouds as it was to try and land under these conditions. Everyone aboard relied on the expertise of the pilot to make it happen. The pilot radioed to the tower, advising that he would be making another approach. Although the landing strip was private, there were attendants standing in the pouring rain, providing an additional light source to aid the pilot in setting the aircraft down. There was no need to notify the cabin that he was going to make another attempt. Roman and the stewardess could feel the plane lowering and the speed of the plane seeming to accelerate.

"Come on, come on, come on," Roman mumbled. He didn't intend for his musings to be audible, but they were, adding a layer of sound against the noise of the storm and the rumblings of the aircraft. Peering out of the window, the blackness of the runway came into view. Water peppered the slick pavement as the landing gear could be heard shifting from the bottom of the jet. The ground moved swiftly as the plane neared the rock-hard surface.

"Come on," Roman whispered again.

The wheels touched the wet pavement, and the plane bumped again. The pilot threw the plane in reverse, attempting to slow it down while maintaining the craft on the slippery surface. The noise from the braking tires was deafening, and the braking didn't seem to end. Although Roman seemed calm, Crystal had her eyes closed tight, whispering a little prayer as the jet moved down the runway. And then, just like that, the jet started to slow and then stop.

"Whew, thank you, Lord," Crystal sighed.

Roman turned in his seat and smiled at his stewardess.

"My sentiments exactly," Roman agreed.

The pilot emerged from the cockpit, just as Roman strode to the front of the aircraft. The two men nodded to each other. They didn't need to say anything more. The door lowered, and the steps descended to the ground. As the sound of the aircraft died, the gentle purr of the Bentley could be heard between thunder rolls. As soon as Roman stepped from the jet, his driver was there, lifting the umbrella over Roman's head to shield him from the storm. Escorting his boss to the awaiting car, the driver opened the door and protected Roman until he was securely inside.

Roman was grateful. And, he was determined.

The driver climbed in the vehicle and awaited his instruction.

"Take me to Ms. Moore's."

Ivory had fallen to sleep not long after her shower and was lulled into a deeper sleep as the rain provided the perfect backdrop. Not even thunder and lightning was enough to wake Ivory from her slumber, not at first. But the loud boom of an especially pronounced round of thunder did rouse her. With sleepy eyes, Ivory rolled over and looked at the clock on her side table. It was nearly midnight. And then Ivory remembered. Roman said he was coming. She wasn't sure where he was traveling from, so she had no sense of how long it would take. But as late as it was, Ivory thought maybe she'd missed his call or maybe he wasn't going to come. That might not be a bad thing, Ivory thought to herself as she still didn't know what she would say to him. Her cell phone sat next to the clock. Ivory reached for it, pulling the phone into the bed with her.

With a swipe to the screen, Ivory saw she'd missed not one but two calls.

"Ugh," she moaned as Ivory repositioned herself beneath the covers. There were two missed calls but only one voice mail. With the press of a button, the automated voicemail came through the line.

*"Hey Ivory. This is your mother."*

Hearing her mom announce herself as though Ivory didn't recognize the voice always made Ivory smile and chuckle a little.

*"I haven't talked to you in a few days. I pray all is well. Dad and I miss you. Call me when you get a chance. Love ya."*

Ivory was still smiling, and she swiped to another screen. She had to check the call log to see what call she missed as whoever it was didn't leave a message.

Ivory looked at the second number. She didn't recognize it. It was too late to call her mother back, and so far, she hadn't heard from Roman. Just as Ivory got ready to set the phone back on the table, she felt it vibrate in her hand. It was a text message.

*I'm on my way to you.*

She didn't have to see the name to know who the message was from.

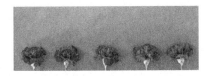

# Chapter Twenty

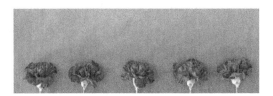

$\mathcal{H}$e was on his way.

Instantly, upon reading the message, Ivory felt the beat of her heart accelerate. She had to take a deep breath to try and slow down the pounding of her heart. Ivory knew Roman to be unrelenting. When he needed to make a point when there was something that he wanted, Roman would not stop until he got what he wanted; whether it was by weakening and exhausting the other person to the point that they caved in or he made a sufficient enough argument that the other person acquiesced. Either way, Roman was known not to give up, to not give in, to fight until the end. As she climbed out of her bed, planting her pedicured feet on the thick rug beside her bed, Ivory wondered if that part of him had changed? And if he hadn't, was she that something he was willing to fight unrelentingly for?

Quietly, Ivory padded to the adjoining bathroom. With the swipe of her hand, she located the light switch illuminating the restroom. As she approached the oval shaped mirror over the pedestal sink, Ivory ran her fingers through her colored tresses. A yawn caused her mouth to open, and Ivory extended her arms high above her head, stretching and inhaling. As her arms lowered to her sides, Ivory looked down at the pajamas she had on. She considered changing, putting on something, 'more appropriate' but quickly decided against it. If Roman was coming, he would have to take her as she was or don't take her at all. Ivory shrugged her shoulders, affirmed in her decision, and then reached out and turned the knobs on the faucet. She waited until the water warmed and then cupped her hands, pooling the water and gently splashing it on her face. Feeling refreshed, Ivory dried her hands and then brushed her teeth. That was all the preparing she intended to do.

Roman's Bentley pulled into the driveway, and the driver put the car in park. It was still raining out, and the driver opened his door, equipped with the umbrella prepared to escort Mr. West to the door. When the back door opened, Roman stepped out and was immediately protected by the vinyl covering.

"I got this," he said to the driver, who handed over the handle of the umbrella to his boss. But unlike others who were catered to, Roman escorted his driver back to the driver side, covering him as he had been covered, until the driver was securely inside.

"Shall I wait?" The driver asked before closing the door.

"No, it's late," Roman replied. "I'll find a way."

He didn't wait for the expected protestation from his

driver. Roman waved to him as he rounded the back of the car, letting his driver know that it was okay to leave.

Just then, she heard her doorbell sound, cracking through the silence that was her house. Again, like before, the beat of Ivory's heart shifted into high gear. And she placed her hand over her chest, feeling the rapid-fire pounding underneath her fingertips. Was nervousness a good sign? She wasn't sure, but Ivory felt a surge of adrenaline pumping through her as she padded towards the front door. There was no question who was waiting on the other side. She knew it was Roman. She knew this would be an encounter that she would not soon forget. The only thing Ivory wasn't certain of was whether the ending would be good or bad.

When Ivory arrived at the door, she turned on the light that illuminated the entryway. Still, the thumping in her chest refused to be quieted. Ivory placed a hand against the door, taking a moment, giving her palpitating heart a chance to calm. On the other side, Roman heard the locks give. Slowly, he lowered the umbrella, standing under the awning that protected him from the rain. His heart was beating fast, too, but Roman used his quickly pulsating heart as fuel, especially after the night he'd already had. When Ivory opened the door, Roman found himself standing there, nearly breathless. She was stunning, effortlessly stunning. His first impulse was to step forward, closing the distance between them, pull her into his arms, and kiss her fully, never letting her go. Roman missed her. Seeing Ivory made Roman feel like he could breathe and that everything, no matter what, was going to be okay. But instead of acting impulsively, Roman took a beat. Impulsivity may have already cost him the relationship he craved. He didn't want to add insult to injury.

"Hey," Ivory uttered as their eyes met. But Ivory didn't hold her gaze too long. She already felt like her heart was beating in her throat, choking off her words. Gazing into Roman's dreamy eyes would only make the situation worse. Ivory took a slight step back and extended her hand, ushering Roman in from the storm. Roman balanced the wet umbrella against the house and stepped across the threshold. As he passed in front of her, Ivory felt a surge of pure energy course through her body, as though the interaction of their auras created a powerful electrical current that passed between them. It was soul-stirring, and a feeling Ivory couldn't deny.

This was going to be hard; harder than she could have imagined. As she closed the door, Ivory talked to herself, encouraging herself to remain calm, level-headed, and to keep her damn legs closed no matter how good Roman made her feel. That bit of chastisement was enough to make Ivory giggle internally, taking a bit of the internalized pressure out of the moment. But only temporarily.

Roman took off his shoes and waited for Ivory to invite him further into her home.

"Let me turn some lights on," Ivory said as she stepped in front of Roman guiding the way. "I didn't realize how dark the house was."

Roman's eyes followed her from the light into the shadows. He waited until Ivory clicked on another light before following behind her. Pivoting on her heels, Ivory welcomed

Roman to the couch, but she didn't sit down next to him. Instead, she stood close by.

"Are you hungry? Thirsty?" Ivory asked.

Roman watched as Ivory wrung her hands and shifted her weight from one foot to the other. He started to ask why she was so nervous, but Roman knew that would only make Ivory more self-conscious.

"No, I'm fine," he started. "But if you want something, help yourself."

Undeniably, Ivory's nerves were getting the best of her. She realized she was fidgeting like a schoolgirl but couldn't make herself stop.

"One second," Ivory suggested, twirling on her heels and padding out of the room. Roman settled in on the couch. He was nervous too, in his own way, but Roman knew he had to hold it together so he wouldn't say or do the wrong thing. He could hear noises coming from the kitchen, and then after a few moments, Ivory reappeared with a bottle of Bordeaux and two wine glasses.

"Just in case," Ivory said, sitting the glasses down and taking a seat on the furthest end of the couch. Before she could get comfortable, Ivory popped up again.

"Shit! I forgot the corkscrew."

Before Roman could say anything, Ivory was gone again, quickly retreating to the kitchen.

*Get yourself together, girl, damn*, Ivory scolded herself. Roman had never made her feel this discombobulated before. Hell, no man did. *You are better than this.* Ivory balanced herself against the granite countertop and harshly exhaled, frustrated with her own flightiness. It was completely out of character and unacceptable. She had to pull it together and quick. Ivory didn't want Roman to think he had that kind of effect on her. She didn't want to look weak and blithering. Ivory blew through her full lips and nodded her head, building herself up and refocusing her energy. Finally, she was ready to go back into the living room with corkscrew in hand.

This time when she returned, Ivory seemed calmer. Her walk was slower and much more graceful as it normally was. Roman didn't miss anything, not when it came to her. She sat down, still on the far end of the sofa, and reached for the wine bottle.

"Let me help you with that," Roman offered.

"Nah," Ivory interjected. "I got it."

She did it with a curt smile, but Roman could see the fire in her eyes. She needed to flex her independence. That was okay with him.

Ivory balanced the bottle between her thighs. The cottony material of her pajama pants was a little slippery at first, but she pressed her thighs firmly together to hold the bottle in place. Roman watched as she picked up the corkscrew and started to work it down into the bottle. She grunted a little as she turned the screw.

"Are you sure you won't let me help?" Roman asked again.

"I got this," Ivory reiterated. This time she wasn't smiling. Instead, she was focused. Her teeth were slightly bared as she pressed the screw down, encouraging the cork to pop.

"Ahh."

Ivory was pleased with herself when the cork finally

released. The smile returned. This time it was a smile of satisfaction. She placed the corkscrew on the table and lifted the bottle from her legs. She poured the dark red wine into one of the glasses and then the other.

"I don't like to drink alone," Ivory quipped. "If I'm gonna make a fool of myself, then you're going to make a fool of yourself right along with me."

Roman accepted the glass Ivory extended to him and held it balanced in his large hand.

"Shall we make a toast?" Roman suggested.

"Sure," Ivory replied, pulling the glass back from her pursed lips. She knew the wine would be liquid courage, the kind of courage she needed for what was to come. But Ivory could live with a momentary delay. "What should we toast to?"

Roman engaged Ivory, waiting until he had her eyes held by his own.

"Us," he crooned, the velvet of his baritone voice piercing through her core.

"Us," Ivory repeated. But there was a lilt to her voice that was as much a question as it was a statement.

"Yes, us," Roman insisted, still maintaining his penetrating gaze.

"What about us," Ivory inquired.

It was getting harder to maintain eye contact with Roman. His brow was hooded, and his piercing dark brown eyes were narrowed by his tightened lids. He loved a challenge, and that's what he heard in Ivory's tone.

"To who we were," Roman began, "and who we're destined to become."

Roman watched as her eyes widened, ever so slightly. Ivory could have commented behind Roman's weighty statement, but she opted not to. Rather, Ivory lifted her glass as did Roman, surprised that she had nothing to say. She kept her eyes on Roman as he lifted the glass to his lips. He paused until she had her glass close to her mouth. Only then did Roman take a sip. Ivory did likewise. But she didn't stop with a dainty sip. The way Ivory was feeling, she drank until the half-filled glass was practically empty, momentarily losing eye contact with Roman.

Before Ivory fully swallowed, she was already reaching for the bottle, refilling her glass. She was starting to feel calmer as the warmth of the dark wine traveled down to her belly. Roman didn't razz her about it. Instead, he was amused as she lifted the glass to her lips without hesitation and took another big sip.

"Let me know when you're ready," Roman chortled. Ivory knew what he meant. He could only resist the temptation to give Ivory a hard time for so long. He hoped his comment would bring a smile to her face. And it did.

"Whenever you are, Mr. West," she quipped. "I'm sure you've practiced what it is you have to say to me."

"Uhm," he moaned, a slight sexily sinister smile lifting the corner of his lips. "Maybe," he retorted.

Ivory chuckled, and her eyes softened. Whether it was the drink or what he said, Roman was glad to see it. He didn't want this to be a tense, awkward moment between them. However, he knew with his next comment, he could make it so. But Roman was willing to take the chance. He had to address the elephant in the room. There was no way around it.

"Because you're that important to me," Roman continued. "So, yes, I practiced," he admitted. "I thought about what I would say, what you might say, and what I would say in return. Because, again, you are important to me, Ivory."

She had no comment behind a statement like that; not a comment that wouldn't sound conjured or disingenuous. She didn't want to be snippy because she knew that Roman meant exactly what he said. He was important to her, too. Ivory sat the glass down on the table. They were at the place, the unavoidable place. She didn't want to play about it or drag it on. Ivory knew if she was ever going to get some mental relief, she would have to deal with this situation head on and honestly, even if it was uncomfortable or made her feel vulnerable in doing so.

# Chapter Twenty-One

$\mathcal{T}$he room fell quiet. The silence was necessary as they both worked through internal thoughts, hoping to articulate them in a way the other would comprehend.

"I don't know what to do with you," Ivory admitted. It was true. She didn't, and that was the crux of her dilemma between her head and her heart.

"What do you want to do with me?"

"I don't know," Ivory whined. "I really don't know." She paused for a minute and thought about his question. "What I really want to do is punch you for being so damn honest, telling me that what I knew of you before wasn't true did something to me." Ivory paused again, this time, fumbling with her fingers, not in a nervous way but in a flustered way. "Telling me that you were in love with me all that time? And I truly didn't have a clue? I don't know, Roman," she confessed. "That made me feel some kind of way like I was blind or stupid or both."

She was so cute when she pouted. He couldn't focus on that, though. Ivory was sharing a piece of her heart with him, and Roman didn't want to minimize how she felt by making light of it. Roman respected what she said. He understood why.

"Not recognizing how you felt about me, made me question just how in tune emotionally I really am."

"Ivory, we were kids then," Roman reasoned. "I did love you; it's true. But that love was to the capacity that I knew how to love then. I didn't say it to you when we were young, because I didn't want to chance feeling differently about me."

Roman leaned over and picked up the wine glass he'd previously sat down. His head lowered, and he absentmindedly traced the rim of the glass with his finger.

"I guess time didn't change that, huh?"

Ivory could hear the disappointment in his voice.

"In some ways, I guess it didn't," Ivory sighed.

"I have to respect that," Roman started, lifting his head to connect with Ivory.

"I guess," he chuckled, but it wasn't a humorous one. "I thought, wow, if by some happenstance, some miracle, the universe gave me a second chance to have you in my life, the right thing to do was be totally honest with you. To let you know the truth about me and what I've always been, not who but what," Roman reasoned. "I thought you would want that, too." Roman shook his head. "I put what I thought was important ahead of our history. Ivory, I can't help but feel responsible for the way that made you feel."

"You are," Ivory sighed.

Some men would have been taken aback by her response. Yet, Roman wasn't. He wanted an honest exchange, no matter what the cost. He had to be willing to hear what it is Ivory had to say, whether it hurt him or not. "But I have some responsibility in feeling the way I do, too," Ivory continued. "Hearing you make the difference between what you are – wealthy, and who you are – Roman...huh..."

Ivory stopped short. Now, she was the one shaking her head. She repeated the phrase in her head, realizing and recognizing the difference, for maybe the first time – who he was versus what he was. If Ivory was honest with herself, had she known Roman was affluent when they were kids, she may have treated him differently, ascribing characteristics and attributes to him that may not have existed. Had his family's status been known from the beginning, they may not have moved in the same circles or had the opportunity to truly get to know the other person for who they were instead of how they could be described. Truthfully, they may have never become friends in the first place. All this time, Ivory had never put herself in Roman's place, considered the situation and the circumstances from his point of view. She had been so focused on her own feelings; she didn't consider his motivation in sharing with her what he shared. And now, knowing his why, shed some light on the situation that Ivory was willing to consider.

Roman sat the glass on the table and moved closer to Ivory, taking her by the hands.

n g

"Listen, my intention was to be real with you, to give you the chance to know me wholly, that's all. And if that changed things for you, I apologize for that, but I felt you of all people, deserved the truth. I didn't say any of those things to push you away or to put you in flux. It's me, babe, me. It's been me all the time. And whether you can't get past it and decide you and I can't move to the next level, I will have no choice but to accept it. That would break my heart. I would be devastated, but I would have to accept it. But let me say this."

Roman's earnest emotions moved through him and spilled over to Ivory, and she felt it, pulsating through the physical connection they had. Looking into Roman's eyes, Ivory saw his heart; the truthfulness and intentions of the man he was. As he spoke, Roman caressed her hands, pouring out his soul to her.

There is one thing that will not change... that's my love for you. For that, Ivory, I will never apologize."

The swell of her heart flushed Ivory's face, and instinctively, she dropped her head.

"Uh uhn," Roman objected, releasing one of her hands to lift her chin gently. "I need you to hear me," he insisted, refusing to allow Ivory to look away.

Roman was willing to wait for her to return his gaze. He needed her to hear and understand what he was saying to her fully.

"Ivory, I love you. You can't change that. I won't let you."

She didn't know what to say. His words soothed her and softened her heart because Ivory felt his heart through his words. She'd never known a man to be more sincere than

Roman, and she felt that deep in her soul. The only thing Ivory could do was accept what he said as truth. What she feared would be a horrible confrontation turned out to be so much more than that, so much better than she could hope for. Ivory reached for him, lacing her arm around Roman's neck. When he released her other hand to pull her close, Ivory was okay with that and rested her head on his shoulder.

A slow deep sigh passed through her lips, and Roman cradled Ivory securely in his arms. He was grateful their conversation had gone as well as it did. It was late, and the toils of a long day started catching up to Roman. His body was tired even though his heart was full. Roman could easily lean back on the couch, with Ivory pressed up against him and fall soundly to sleep. Roman lifted his hand and covered his mouth as he yawned.

"You must be tired," Ivory whispered, the warmth of her breath tickling the thick of his neck. But she didn't lift herself from him; instead, snuggling up closer, holding on to him tighter.

"I am," Roman answered. "It's been a long day."

"It's late," Roman crooned. "I better go."

This time, Ivory did lift her head. "Is your driver waiting for you?"

"No," Roman replied. "I let him go home. I'll just call for a car."

"It's too late at night for that," Ivory replied. "Roman, you're more than welcome to stay here."

"Are you sure?"

"Yes," Ivory smiled. "I'm sure."

Roman pulled slightly back so he could look into Ivory's eyes.

"Are you sure?"

She smiled again. "Yes, Roman, I'm sure." Ivory chuckled.

"No pressure," he whispered as he stood to his feet, lifting her with him. Roman reached for her hand and led her to the bedroom. Roman disrobed, relieving himself of his formal attire, leaving on his t-shirt and boxers. Then, he kissed Ivory lightly at first and then more deeply. He enveloped Ivory in his strong arms, and she melted. Disengaging from his lips, Ivory turned to face the bed and eased the covers back. She climbed in, not exactly sure what to do next. Roman climbed in next to Ivory and eased her down into him, his chest to her back. Her breathing was tentative, and her heart fluttered.

"... no pressure..." he whispered again, reassuring Ivory.

"... no pressure..."

She breathed deeper, allowing herself to relax and trust him at his word. He pulled Ivory closer; their bodies completely connected; his physical indistinguishable from her own. As they lay there, holding each other, his inhale began to match her inhale; his exhale aligned with hers. And before long, Ivory felt a gentle rumbling in his chest and the soft sounds of a man in slumber. She laid there for the longest time, listening to him, feeling him, enjoying him. When sleep finally came, there was a smile on Ivory's lips.

Ivory awoke the next morning to still feel Roman's arms wrapped tightly around her waist. He stirred, and after greeting Ivory with a gentle kiss to her neck, Roman coaxed her over, and they were face to face.

"Good morning, beautiful," he cooed.

"Good morning, beloved."

Have you ever woken up to someone who instantly made you feel all warm and tingly inside? Well, that's how Ivory felt looking up at him. She knew she had the biggest, goofiest smile on her face. And Roman smiled, too. That made her smile even more. She reached up and wrapped both arms around his neck and hugged him for making her feel so good by simply being there. As they separated, the giddy feelings turned into something else. There was an internal heat that began to echo throughout her body. She placed one hand gently on each side of Roman's ruggedly handsome face and marveled. She looked deeply into his eyes, and his gaze penetrated hers. Their faces were not even an inch apart, not touching but close enough to feel the vibration that flowed between them. Roman was conscious, awakened, and it lured Ivory like bees to honey. The seduction was not physical. It was mental and heart-full and soulful.

So, when he eased Ivory down into the bed, there was no hesitation, no reluctance, and no fear. Before he moved a step further, Roman checked in with Ivory. He didn't say anything; he didn't have to. There was a slight raise to his eyebrows and his face; his eyes were sincere. She answered affirmatively with a passionate kiss to his inviting lips. Ivory appreciated Roman; he took his time with her, passionately bringing out the woman in her. Roman undressed her and then himself. Roman's eyes lowered, appreciating the swell of her beautiful breasts. He regarded them as though they were delicate; tracing their fullness with his fingers and titillating Ivory's nipples first with his hands and then with light kisses.

She'd been sexually aroused before but nothing like this. There was a quickening inside Ivory. Her breathing sped up, and her heart drummed steadily in her chest. Whatever thoughts she had in her mind before Roman touched her evaporated into nothingness. Ivory's mind was a blank canvas slowly being colored in by Roman's caress. As his lips found her mounds and he suckled, the sounds that escaped her lips refused to be contained. She looked down at him, and he looked up at her, and Ivory's heart melted just a little bit more. She caressed his head as his mouth traced from her breasts down her center. Ivory felt his manhood rising as his body pressed ever so slightly against her. Another rush of warmness surged through the entirety of her body.

Roman began to ease Ivory's panties down on one side and then the other. She lifted her hips slightly so he could fully remove them. She thought, considering how their relationship began, being the best of friends, she would have been more hesitant to give herself to him fully. Maybe there would have been more hesitancy, doubt, fear that maybe she was making the wrong decision, completely ruining what they had, or maybe he wasn't the right man or a whole host of other things. But none of that was true in that moment. To say Ivory was calm wouldn't be exactly accurate because her body physically pulsated; it had truly come alive. She felt sensations she'd never felt before. So calm is not the right word. But, she was at peace... she was peaceful in her decision.

Again, Roman took a moment to look at what was newly

exposed. He didn't immediately touch her there, just appreciating the deliciousness of her jewel with his eyes and then slowly tracing the edges with his fingers. As though pulled by a puppet's string, Ivory's back arched, leaving the cool sheets temporarily vacated. Roman eased up beside her and then leaned over the side of the bed. He turned back towards her with a condom in hand. There was this light moment that briefly broke the intensity, but it was short lived. She watched as Roman eased his boxers off and her eyes were transfixed when she saw his manhood strong and erect.

Roman saw Ivory's reaction, and there was a smirk of a smile. He took his free hand and reached for her hand. She acquiesced, and he led Ivory's hand to touch him there. She was like a child tempted to touch a flickering flame; yet, Ivory's womanhood throbbed from yearning. She wanted him inside her in the worst way and the moan that passed through her lips told him so. He was thick and firm and when she touched him, Roman crooned a guttural grown that sent chills down her core. Her pussy thumped again. Ivory's body yearned for an even greater touch from him.

She pulled him towards her saying yes with her body. He kissed her deeply, and Ivory's legs gave way. Roman lifted his lips from her lips, and once again, their eyes locked intensely. She felt the sting and then prick of his manly entrance into her. Ssss... oooohhh... ahhhh... The cherry of Ivory's juices erupted with his first touch coating him completely, making his first thrust smooth. Her head fell back between the blades of her shoulders as his manly strength covered her.

They were no longer just friends...

The pleasure came in waves; first long and smooth as Roman stroked her puss deep, but crashing just the same. The thickness of his manhood filled Ivory completely, and he hit her g spot with exactness that made her squeal in ecstasy. She couldn't help it. And then the intensity of the waves increased as the tempo of their fuck increased; sweat peppered his brow, their thighs slapping together with every upward thrust, the animalistic moans spilling from both of their lips as they lost themselves in each other's passion. His eyes never left Ivory as they found a syncopated rhythm, his drum to her drum, echoed by the rod iron headboard banging relentlessly against the wall like a bass drum. Ivory traced Roman's body down to the small of his back, and with his next thrust, he lifted her to a height she never felt before.

"Ahh, Roman, shit," she uttered breathlessly.

Her nails sunk into his skin, and the pleasure of her jewel mixed with the sting in his back pushed a guttural utterance from his lips that sent shockwaves through Ivory. Roman's warm breath heated her as he whispered against her ear, calling her name.

"Ivory..."

She didn't know how long they were in that space because she lost track of time. The beat of Ivory's heart pounded so loudly in her ears it was deafening. Her body was wet with his sweat comingled with hers, and the headboard crashed hard against the wall. Every time he thought about how much he loved her, how long he had loved her, Roman couldn't contain it. He had craved Ivory for so long, not just her body, but connecting with her soul, giving himself fully to her, letting her know that she meant everything and more to him. He was breathless, overcome, and primal. Roman needed to see if she knew if she felt the same. He had to gain her eyes so he could peer into the depths of her soul. And she was right there, waiting for him, her beautiful eyes gazing back at him without hesitation. Ivory saw him, not as the little boy from her past, not as her junior high school bestie, but she saw him totally - the man he was today. They felt the connection. It was more than either of them could ever imagine. It was transcendental, mind blowing, heartfelt, soul stirring. That drove Roman nearly to the brink. His heart couldn't take much more.

"Bae," he moaned.

Their eyes stayed connected as the heat and passion rose to an astrological level. Roman wrapped his arms around Ivory, lifting her to him. She felt his body quaking as he moved deeply inside her. Ivory wrapped her legs around him, never wanting to let Roman go. The realization of that brought tears to Ivory's eyes. She didn't want to let him go. She wanted what he wanted for her. The powerful thrusts grew faster, and she felt his manhood swell inside her walls. Ivory panted, unable to catch her breath. The banging of the headboard against the wall grew to a fevered pounding as their hearts raised and Roman exploded inside her.

"Uhhhhh," he growled, dropping his head into her bosom. They melded together like one person, Ivory's body being physically lifted from the bed from the power of the man moving inside her. They breathed and connected and shared and loved and exploded all in the same space.

There were more waves and aftershocks as Ivory's body couldn't squelch the internal explosions. Roman held her snugly against his beautiful body. Finally, they both collapsed, exhausted. The rise and falls of their chests were still fast-paced and could barely be quieted. Ivory reached up and brushed her curly tresses away from her face. Her eyes rolled to the top of her head as she tried to level her breathing. And then, unexpectedly, she started to giggle.

Roman's hand found her waist as his eyes opened.

"What's funny," he asked, still panting.

"Look up," Ivory said, pointing just overhead. She couldn't stop giggling, and Roman was intrigued.

Roman's eyes followed Ivory's finger, and then he rolled over on his muscled belly to get a better look.

"Damn," Roman groaned, shaking his head and smirking at the same time.

"Yep," Ivory affirmed, giggling even more. "You done broke the wall."

They both fell out in a fit of laughter.

"I love your crazy ass," Ivory giggled. And then hearing what she said, her eyes widened, and the laughter softened on her lips. He didn't miss it, though. Roman felt like he had waited his entire life to hear those three magical words. And coming from Ivory, the truest love of his life, they were absolutely magical.

"Say it again," Roman encouraged, zeroing in on her beautiful face and focusing on her full lips. Ivory felt warmth pouring into her cheeks. She couldn't contain the smile that danced at the corner of her lips, no matter how hard she tried. Hearing herself say it wasn't as scary as she thought it would be. Ivory knew it at some level. She tried to mask it, deny it, not trust it; yet, that feeling was there. Ivory no longer wanted to deny what her heart and soul truly felt. Her mind? She controlled, and Ivory refused to allow intellect or fear, more honestly, direct her actions or inactions.

"I love you, Roman West," she mused. It was as much an affirmation for him as it was for herself. "I do," she grinned. "I love you."

Roman couldn't hold back the smile that emerged on his face. Her announced love was more than music to his ears. Leaning in, Roman kissed Ivory lightly on the lips and then lifted his mouth, kissing her on the forehead. Roman's mouth lingered there, feeling a powerful connection to the woman who stole his heart. Ivory cupped his handsome face in her hands and held them there. The connection she felt in the quietness of that moment gave Ivory extreme resolve. She felt so at peace. It was amazing. Roman lowered himself and reengaged Ivory's eyes. He felt her gaze wash over him. She saw him, who he was in the present, and Roman felt that in his spirit.

"I love you, too, bae," Roman said, kissing her lips again. "Always have," he kissed her again, "always will."

# Chapter Twenty-Two

THREE MONTHS LATER

*T*hat night was incredibly special for Ivory and Roman. That night led to many other nights of the two enjoying each other's company, spending quality time together, laughing, talking, and for Ivory, being comfortable loving the man she realized she loved. But the world didn't stop turning, nor their individual obligations diminish simply because they were in love. Roman still maintained an incredibly hectic traveling scheduling tending to his family's businesses. Ivory's post at the Sudanese Embassy continued to be demanding as the push for social justice in the Diplomat's home country revved up. When they were apart, they spent long nights on the phone talking about any and everything. So much of it was like it had been in the past, where no subject was off limits. Ivory had always been attracted to intelligence. Roman was that. Some of their most engaging conversations were on topics with which they disagreed. She loved to hear Roman wax eloquently and passionately about his point of view. And despite her own level of intellect, Ivory loved it when she learned something new from him. Ivory was a true sapiosexual and mental stimulation was a powerful aphrodisiac. What made Ivory and Roman's connection even more powerful, was that he felt the same way, invigorated by her brilliance and energized from her expressiveness.

It felt so good just to laugh, with no pretention, no pomp or circumstance, just pure unadulterated laughter. Roman kept Ivory laughing. Her laughter was a sound he couldn't get enough of, and if he could brighten her day with a corny joke, that's exactly what Roman would do.

"I want you to be happy," he would say. "Even if it's at my expense."

Although initially, Ivory had been trepidatious, wary when it came to matters of her heart, she realized that walling her heart away for fear of heartbreak was also walling herself away from what could be good for her. Sometimes you have to push the boundaries of your comfort zone and take a risk, even if that risk means exposing your heart to another. From the moment Ivory realized she loved Roman, and finally was able to tell him so, she never regretted taking that leap of faith. Could Ivory end up being hurt, disappointed, heartbroken? She could. But Ivory refused to spend energy worrying about the possibilities. She was willing to give her relationship with Roman the best possible chance.

The one thing Roman and Ivory continued to disagree about was his desire to surprise her.

"Explain it to me," Roman asked in the wee hours of the morning when they were on the phone.

Ivory shifted uncomfortably in her bed. "Can we talk about something else?"

"No," Roman rebuffed without hesitation. "Seriously, babe, I want to understand.

"Because," Ivory groaned.

"That's not a reason," Roman challenged. "Talk to me," Roman encouraged as he stood next to a picture window in the penthouse suite, he currently occupied. Like Las Vegas, Atlanta was a city that rarely slept. Even at this hour, there were some cars moving through the city streets and even a few pedestrians ambling down the walkways.

"Why can't you just not do it?" Ivory challenged.

He liked her stubbornness. That just made Roman even more intrigued. He would offer an explanation, even though he knew it was merely a stall tactic on Ivory's part. Roman was willing to play along for the moment.

"You know the answer," Roman iterated. Now, answer my question?"

Ivory knew full well that once Roman got hold of a notion, he wouldn't let it go. But even with someone, she knew so well, admission could be difficult.

"I like to be in control," Ivory quietly admitted.

When Roman moaned a low guttural moan that sent a swirl of chills up her spine, Ivory felt a pulsation in her puss, reminiscent of how she felt when his tongue stroked her jewel. Ivory squirmed underneath the sheet, readjusting her body to accommodate the quickening sensation she felt in her core.

"What's that all about?" Ivory asked, defying the thump between her thighs.

"The thought of you being in control," Roman trilled, his sensual voice rumbling.

"You nasty," Ivory squealed with laughter.

"You like it," Roman rebuffed. They were both wearing flirty smiles.

"I need to be there with you," Roman crooned.

"Oh really," Ivory purred.

"Mmhmm," he affirmed. "You can be in charge," Roman suggested.

"Roman, don't you bring your ass over here," Ivory teased. "Some of us have to work in the morning," she said and then quickly added, "for other people."

Roman chuckled. "Okay," he agreed, not missing her snarky caveat. "I'll let you do your thing, but don't be surprised when I show up."

Ivory knew that wasn't a threat. Coming from Roman, Ivory knew it was a promise.

ALTHOUGH IVORY SPENT MOST OF THE NIGHT ON THE telephone with Roman, she still had to be at work early. And as usual, the day was filled with meetings, telephone conferences to dignitaries around the world who were stakeholders in the fight for the Sudanese women, and hours of translation, both written and verbal. The work was invigorating, yet at the end of a fourteen-hour day, Ivory was exhausted. She did manage, however, to offer a smile to the security guard who made sure to greet her and wish her a good rest of the evening every time he saw her. No matter how tired or preoccupied Ivory may have been, the continued pleasantness of the guard always put a smile on her face.

As she exited the embassy, Ivory's only thought was getting to her car, getting home, and kicking off her shoes. Just then, Ivory heard a high-pitched whistle. She'd been catcalled before and promptly ignored it. Her stride remained unchanged as she made her way to the covered garage. All Roman could do was chuckle as his long strides took him across the front of the embassy towards where Ivory was walking.

"Excuse me, Ms. lady," Roman cooed, walking up slightly behind her. Ivory spun on her heels so fast, prepped and ready to let whoever the man was have it. Roman knew he was taking a risk, but seeing Ivory's eyes go from narrowed and tight to wide with surprise was absolutely worth it.

"Ugh! Dammit, Roman!"

He braced himself for the punch he knew was coming. And swing Ivory did. Her heart was pumping so hard in her chest.

"Come here, girl," Roman said, coaxing Ivory into his thick arms.

"You scared the shit out of me," Ivory fussed as she was enveloped by the bear hug he put on her.

"Whew, that mouth," Roman playfully scolded. "Let me kiss it."

Ivory was still fussing when Roman's enticing mouth captured her lips sweetly at first and then more fully, stealing the words she intended to say. Initially, Ivory was still salty when Roman first kissed her. But it didn't take long for her anger to subside, and her mouth and body respond to his magical touch.

"I'm sorry," Roman offered. He spoke the words against Ivory's lips, warming them even more. "Do you forgive me?"

"Nope," Ivory quipped, their lips still touching.

"Please," Roman implored, nibbling and kissing Ivory's pouty lips.

"Uh huhn," Ivory protested.

"Please, babe," Roman asked. "I promise I'll make it up to you."

He kissed her lips again, soft sweet kisses, tracing the natural shape of her mouth. Ivory's resistance was fleeting. He tasted so good to her.

"Hmph," she scoffed. "You've got a lot of making up to do."

"Promise?" Roman smiled against her mouth.

"You are the worst," Ivory giggled. "The worst."

"Yet, you love me, don't you?" Roman crooned, trailing steaming kisses from Ivory's wanton lips down the elegance of her neck. She moaned in response, although she tried to stay tough.

"You make me so sick," Ivory purred as a sexy smile, entranced her lips.

"I love you, too," Roman guffawed, kissing her neck

again, this time, pulling and sucking against the pulsations that beat underneath his lips. Although the tugging pulled on her yoni, when Ivory realized what he was doing, she couldn't help but laugh and fuss even more.

"A hickie Roman, seriously? That is so old school," Ivory giggled, and then shook her head in disbelief.

"I've waited a helluva long time to do that," he hummed, smiling.

"What am I going to do with you," Ivory smiled, leaning back so she could see Roman's handsome face.

"Whatever you want to," he mused with hooded eyes.

"Remember, you said that, okay?" Ivory teased.

"Girl," Roman chortled. He didn't need to say more, his eyes, his mouth, the way he held her said it all. "Come on," Roman said. "I've got something I want you to see."

Roman took a step to the side and pulled Ivory in close under his arm. But before he could take a step forward, Ivory halted, sliding her hand up her ample hip and leveling Roman with a heated gaze.

"What?" Ivory challenged. "I thought we had an under-standing?"

"We do, babe," Roman countered with an alluring smile. "I'm giving you every chance to be in control. I can't wait for it."

Ivory knew dealing with Roman on this issue was a lost cause.

"Fine, I gotchu," Ivory quipped. "Just make sure you're ready for what you've been waiting for."

"I love it when you talk dirty," Roman hummed, leaning down and whispering in her ear.

Ivory threw her head back, laughing. She couldn't be mad at him for too long. He always managed to find a way to make her laugh and feel sexy and desired at the same time. Ivory was willing to move and the two fell in step, heading towards Roman's vehicle.

"What about my car?" Ivory asked as the driver stepped around back to open the back passenger door.

"I'll take care of it," Roman reassured, asking for her car keys. "It will be at your house by the time you get home."

"You think of everything, don't you?"

"Yes," Roman agreed, "especially when it comes to you."

He turned to his driver, handing him the keys. "Take Ms. Moore's car to her house."

"Absolutely," the driver replied, accepting the keys. Relinquished of his responsibilities, the driver made his way to the covered garage.

"Here, babe," Roman said, opening the front door. "I want you next to me."

Ivory acquiesced, sliding into the front seat of the silver on silver Rolls Royce. Quickly, she melded into the buttery leather seat, as Roman closed the door. He moved to the driver's side and climbed in, adjusting the seat to accommodate his length.

"I won't even ask where you're taking me," Ivory said, resting her elbow on the comfortable arm rest. Roman reached for her hand, and Ivory willingly folded hers into his. He offered Ivory a wink and a smile as he pulled the Rolls from the curb. With soft jazz playing in the background, the two rode quietly to the destination Roman had in mind. The quiet was just as comfortable as their conversation always was. It had been that way ever since Ivory acknowledged how she truly felt about Roman and accepted him for the man he was. She knew, undoubtedly, that he loved her without condition. That was something she'd never had before, and it was nice.

As they navigated through the Atlanta streets, things became very familiar. Ivory looked out of the passenger side window, starting to get a notion of where they were going. When Roman turned the last corner, and their old middle school came into view, all Ivory could do was smile. And when Roman pulled the Rolls up to the front door and stopped the vehicle, Ivory laughed, shaking her head.

"Wow," she uttered. "I haven't been here in forever."

As always, seeing the smile on Ivory's face made Roman's heart smile.

"Why are we here," Ivory asked, turning her attention back to Roman.

"I thought it would be fun to see our old stomping grounds," he answered.

"Nice," Ivory smiled, thinking to herself, this surprise isn't so bad. She was actually relieved and willingly stepped out of the vehicle when Roman extended his hand.

The school was vacated, as all the scholars were gone for the day, but for Roman, accommodations had been made giving him access. Just being back on campus put Ivory in a nostalgic mood, so many fond memories of her pre-teen years.

"The hallways still smell the same," Ivory chuckled, wrinkling her nose as they walked down the main corridor.

"Some things never change," Roman added as he walked

a half-step behind her. Ivory meandered down the hallway, pointing at classrooms they once occupied together and cut up in. She was all smiles, and her laughter echoed down the long thoroughfare.

"The trophy case," Ivory squealed, clapping her hands.

"How did I know you were going to stop here," Roman chuffed, walking up behind her and peering into the glass.

Ivory giggled and clapped her hands, quickly pointing out the golden trophies with her name finely etched in the plate. There were several, some demonstrating Ivory's athletic prowess, while others showed off her intellectual resilience.

"Roman, babe, did I miss the <u>one</u> with your name on it?" She asked teasingly.

"I'm sure it's still there," Roman scoffed, bending slightly, attempting to locate his memorabilia.

Ivory lifted onto her heels, exaggerating the movement and then bending over, placing her hand to her forehead as if she was looking a long distance. She giggled the entire time.

"Oh, you got jokes, huh," Roman chortled, stepping behind Ivory and lifting her off her feet, stepping back and swinging her in the air.

"Woooo," Ivory guffawed as he spun her around. After a few rounds, Roman sat Ivory down safely on her feet.

"I'm sorry, babe," she giggled, unable to contain herself. "I couldn't see it."

"Mmhmm," Roman huffed, reaching for her hand, which she accepted. They were still in high spirits as they meandered further down the hallway.

"Aw," Ivory sighed as they turned the corner. "My locker is right up there."

"Sure is," Roman agreed.

They walked together, hand in hand, to an old familiar spot. They hung out by Ivory's locker every chance they got. And Roman reminisced about those times he waited for her there between classes, always smiling when she arrived.

"Man," Ivory mused. "This brings back memories, doesn't it?"

"Absolutely," Roman agreed. "Do you remember wearing your locker key around your neck like it was a keepsake?"

"We all did, well the girls anyway," Ivory replied. "That key was special," Ivory reminisced. "It opened your own little personal space. It didn't just hold your books and stuff, but your mirror, picture of your bestie and your boyfriend... all kinds of important things," Ivory explained. She turned on her heels and faced Roman. "Even after we moved on to high school, I still had that key."

"Where is it now," Roman asked.

"I have no idea," Ivory thought. "None whatsoever."

Roman eased his hand into his pants pocket. When he turned his hand over and opened it, Ivory was stunned.

"What??" She gasped. "Are you kidding me right now?"

It was the key to her old locker, still sporting the silver chain she wore around her neck.

"How in the world," Ivory asked, lifting the key from his hand and examining it closely.

"Your mom helped," Roman explained.

"I should have known," Ivory laughed. "She don't throw nothin' away."

"See if it works," Roman suggested.

"Now you know this ain't gone work," Ivory chided.

"Just try, babe," he encouraged again.

"Fine," Ivory huffed with a smile. "Im'ma do it just so I can prove to you that it's not going to work."

Ivory spun around again, this time to face the locker. She cast a sideways look over her shoulder, making sure Roman was watching so he could see the moment she proved she was right. Carefully, Ivory slid the key into the lock, sure it wouldn't turn. Then, she felt it just as she heard it. The tumbler of the lock released and clicked.

Ivory turned around wide eyed with her mouth slightly ajar. "No freakin' way!"

"Open it," Roman crooned with a knowing smile. Ivory paused, examining Roman's eyes.

"What did you do," she questioned, realizing that just being back in their old stomping grounds was not the real surprise.

"Just open it, bae."

Ivory felt an unexpected escalation in the beat of her heart. Suddenly she was nervous and felt queasy in her belly.

"Please," Roman encouraged, seeing the light partially fade from her eyes. He could tell Ivory was curious but also cautious. He knew how much she hated being surprised. But for him, there was no other way to do it. He would certainly make it up to her later. He'd already promised her that.

She huffed, her cheeks expanding and then slowly returning to normal. Ivory knew he wouldn't let her out of it, so she did what he asked just to get it over with. Reaching for the handle, she slowly lifted it and pulled the locker door open. Once again, her eyes widened, and her mouth fell open as her eyes fell onto a small black box. Roman watched as Ivory's head dropped and he could see her body begin to shake. He moved up behind her, pressing his flesh to hers, reassuring Ivory that he was there. Reaching around her, Roman picked up the box but didn't insist that she move. His heart was pounding in his chest too. It had taken everything in him not to show just how nervous he had been the entire time. So, they both took a moment, breathing together.

After a moment, Roman turned Ivory in his arms so he could see her face. He needed to see her, and he wanted Ivory to see him, too. When he lifted her chin to meet her eyes, a tear teetered on her lid. Gently, Roman wiped it away and then kissed her on the cheek where her tear would have fallen.

"I couldn't think of a better place to remind me just how long I've loved you," Roman began. "I have loved you, Ivory, more than half my life, but never more than this moment right now. You mean everything to me, everything. And to know that you love me back? That's all I'll ever need. I understand why you don't like surprises. I think it's because you couldn't trust that the person surprising you only wanted the best for you. That's what I want for you and promise to give you. I understand that surprises make you feel out of control. Just know, you can lose control with me because I'll never use it against you. I'm your safe place, me, and I want to be that for you for as long as I live."

The tears flowed freely as Ivory listened to what Roman

had to say. There was such a pull on her heart that she couldn't stop the tears from flowing.

"I cannot imagine living the rest of my life without you. I don't want to," Roman continued, lowering himself to one knee. Ivory gasped, covering her mouth with both hands. "That's why I need you to say yes, Ivory. Say yes to being my wife. Say yes to making my dreams come true. Say yes to a lifetime of a man working every day to love you like you've never been loved; to treat you like the precious gift that you are, to support you, honor you and surprise you even though you hate it."

Roman opened the box and took out the ring; a six-carat pear shaped diamond with a one carat diamond band. Ivory could barely see it through her tear- filled eyes.

"Ivory Rose Moore, will you be my wife?"

She could barely breathe; Ivory was so overwhelmed. Looking into Roman's eyes, she could see his heart.

All she could manage was a nod of the head as she wiped the tears running down her cheeks.

"Is that a yes," Roman asked, nervously awaiting her reply.

"Mmhmm," Ivory muttered, still nodding. "Yes, yes, Roman, yes."

Roman stood to his feet and eased the ring onto her finger.

"It's beautiful," Ivory sighed.

"A mere reflection of you," Roman crooned. He pulled Ivory into his arms. Her yes made Roman the happiest man in the world. Roman held on to her like he never wanted to let her go. And he didn't. He never wanted to let Ivory go;

feeling her heartbeat against him, feeling the warmth of how she held him, the feeling was one Roman knew would never get old.

As the two made their way towards the entrance, hand in hand, Roman had one more thing he needed to say.

"I'm so glad you said yes," he mused as he smiled looking down at Ivory.

"Did you think I wouldn't," she asked.

"I prayed that you would," Roman replied. "Because sometimes," Roman sighed.

"Sometimes what?" Ivory guffawed, bumping her shoulder into him. She was still elated and the smile she wore said so.

Roman reeled her in again, holding her close. "Because sometimes, you can be stubborn, and mean and surly," Roman teased.

"Nuhn uhn," Ivory objected. Her arched brows knocked together and her pouty lips turned downwards.

Roman paused their steps and centered Ivory in front of him. He ran his hand fingers through the curl of her natural afro and then centered his hold on her to the center of her back.

"I know it's because you've had to be careful, discerning and protective with your heart."

"That sounds better," Ivory sighed, looking up into his deep, brooding eyes.

"But if you said no, I would have a lot of explaining to do," Roman commented as they turned and trekked the last few feet to the front door.

"Explaining?" Ivory asked, a little befuddled. "To whom?"

Roman opened the door to the school. "To them."

Ivory was still focused on Roman when the door opened. Then, her gaze drifted to where his eyes were inclined. Roman dropped his gaze to see her reaction as Ivory witnessed her entire family standing in front of the school with dozens of roses and celebratory balloons. They were all there to celebrate with her. Roman watched as her eyes widened with surprise. Ivory's hands went to cover her mouth. And then, her brow furrowed, and her face wrinkled as the incredible sight sunk into her soul. They were all there to celebrate with her. Tears stung the back of her eyes as she and Roman descended the stairs. Ivory's tears fell to her cheeks as she approached her mother who was already crying.

"Congratulations, baby," Felicia sighed as she hugged and kissed her daughter. "I'm so happy for you."

"Sissy!" Trinity squealed, joining in on the hug.

Congratulations and well wishes were shared by everyone as they encircled the couple. Her sisters were crying. Her brothers-in-law welcomed Roman to the family. Ivory's dad was doing his best not to shed a tear. It was a magical moment.

With Roman standing by her side and all her family around, Ivory knew she was truly loved. It was more than she could have ever dreamed.

*The End*

READING FAMILY, THANK YOU SO MUCH FOR READING MOORE Than Enough. Can you believe it! We only have one more Moore sister left! This ride has been incredible, and I am so glad you decided to join me on this journey. I loved writing this book, and I hope you loved it! I would really appreciate it, especially if you enjoyed the story if you would leave a review on Amazon and Goodreads. For Indie authors, reviews are the lifeblood of our work. They give other readers insight into the story and greater visibility for the authors. Thanks in advance, and I hope you will continue reading the Moore Friends Series with me!

Coming soon!

If you haven't already, please check out,
Other Books Written by Celeste:

All That & Moore Series:

Hidden Missing Moore

I Am Moore

Teach Me Moore

Expect Moore

So Much Moore

Never Moore

I Found Moore

Promise Me Moore

Moore to Love Series:

Stipulations

Gabriel's Melody

Temptations


MOORE FRIENDS SERIES:

Something New

A Love So New

Before I Fall

Falling

Lady Guardians Series:
Onyx Rides
Cruisin'
Curvalicious


Want to be in the know? Subscribe to my newsletter to be a part of Celeste Granger's Tangled Romance!

HTTPS://LANDING.MAILERLITE.COM/WEBFORMS/LANDING/K2EIJ4

Join my Reading Group! https://www.facebook.com/groups/1943300475969127/

Follow me on Facebook @ https://www.facebook.com/TheCelesteGranger/

$14.99

$14.99

Made in the USA
Middletown, DE
22 April 2025

74623834R00136